DRUIDS

"Cinematic in scope and style, DRUIDS illuminates a people clouded in magic and dark legend. A stand-out in fantasy fiction."

—Peter Filardi– prominent Hollywood screenwriter

DRUIDS

By

Nicholoas Checker

Oak Tree Press Hanford, CA

Oak Tree Press
Publishers Since 1998

For information, address Oak Tree Press, 1820 W. Lacey Boulevard, Suite 220, Hanford, CA 93230.

Oak Tree Press books may be purchased for educational, business, or sales promotional purposes. Contact Publisher for quantity discounts.

First Edition, September 2014

ISBN 978 1-61009-124-4
LCCN 2013948223

Dedication

To the memory of both my parents who imbued in me a passion for storytelling and for reading. And to the memory of Kathy Sprinkle, who passed away far too young, and whose spirit runs through the character of the young healer Kirspen in this story.

Acknowledgments

The Morehouse family (my guardian angels)for the long ago gift of the Writer's Handbook which prompted me into writing for publication, and for their eternal faith and support in *all* my endeavors; early readers of my new works – Steve and Cheryl Loyd, Tim Valliere, Anna Sullivan – who always took the time to look at my material and comment on it; my nephew Harold Joyce for his unwavering faith and support when most needed; my family and friends who have always lent support; artist Katie Loyd for her beautiful cover design; my students over the years for their steadfast loyalty and faith; David Tetzlaff, who provided me with the technological means of resurrecting my past literary works from the archives and bringing them back to life; Hollywood screenwriters Jason and Peter Filardi who encouraged me to convert DRUIDS from an earlier screenplay format into its current novel form; my local media; and finally – my gracious publisher, Billie Johnson, and the entire staff of Oak Tree Press for believing in my work. Thanks to all!

The Druid's *Sense*

"I sometimes felt strange things
happening inside me, especially
when I walked in the woods. The
voices of the animals and the birds ...
they were like *songs* in my head.
I could nearly understand them.
And sometimes it seemed as if the
trees all around me ... even the
rocks ... the ground itself was
so ... *active*. I know now, from
Duwin, that those were my first
experiences with the *Living Energy*.
Druids believe it exists in all things."

—Turi, druid acolyte

CHAPTER ONE

Breach!

Hordes of foot soldiers and knights stormed the battered walls of Castle Kathor, the attacking army flanked by hooded druids waving their arms and shrieking incantations into the bitter night. Fiery bolts raked the sky; catapults hurled huge rocks toward the walls; and archers sent waves of arrows raining down on castle defenders. It appeared Kryzol, the Druid-King of Dekras, would make good on his vow to bring ruin upon the realm of his estranged cousin, Queen Shaikela.

The robed figure of a woman was poised majestically on the castle's battlements — her arms spread wide, one hand clutching a long, glowing dagger that deflected many of the incoming bolts. Though stronger in her use of the Cryptic Sense than her cousin Kryzol, Shaikela knew that Kathor lacked the armed forces to contend with his superior legions. The castle could not hold much longer.

It was a war most folk believed should never have taken place.

* * *

The Druid-King had long denounced the nomadic tribes that had dared settle along his southern borders as *squatters*: "Invasive seedlings capable of swelling into a budding foreign threat!" And when some indeed grew into villages and hamlets – a few evolving gradually into minor kingdoms – it alarmed him, in particular the ones who opposed his insistence that they show a benign intent by embracing the mysterious cultural ways of Dekras. Kryzol proclaimed there was "No threat if they conducted themselves as true vassal colonies." Some bowed fearfully to the Druid-King's "request"; others resisted. One such resistor was King Kieman of Kathor, prominent in the South. He had felt their dwelling far across the Old Tundra from Dekras had already made their benign intent sufficiently clear. Kieman insisted that being such a lengthy distance away afforded them the liberty of living independent of "Kryzol and his brooding folk to the North."

The Druid-King disagreed and responded with what he had believed to be a sly stroke of cunning. Kryzol sent his beautiful young cousin Shaikela, a gifted druidess, across the Old Tundra to visit Kathor and to bedazzle its unmarried king. And though King Kieman was a good deal older – well into his middle-aged years and not a particularly attractive man – Shaikela, instead, fell to loving him and his wistful ways of tasting life's fruits. Kryzol's intent to see the King of Kathor hopelessly smitten with the young beauty had not included her feeling the same way about a somewhat homely man nearly old enough to be her father.

The announcement of plans for a royal wedding, not long after, had done even less to comfort Kryzol who had secretly fancied his young cousin. It also gave him cause to fear a brewing rebellion from "an obstinate people who might one day challenge Dekras for mastery of the Old Tundra Lands." So when Shaikela disobeyed Kryzol's demand that she renounce her betrothal to Kathor's king – and went ahead with her marriage to the very man he had sent her to ensnare – the Druid-King of Dekras fell into a rage. Thus began a savage war that could end only with the capture or death of either king.

* * *

Return arrows, spears, and rocks flew out from behind the turreted walls at the intruding army, while hot scalding oil was poured down to deter attackers from scaling the walls on makeshift ladders. Even so, a number of the enemy foot soldiers scrambled their way up and over the main gate barriers. They were immediately engaged by Castle Kathor's knights and other defenders armed with swords, pikes and spears. Dekras soldiers garbed in bright maroon hurled themselves recklessly at those wearing the leafy green of Kathor.

A burly rooster of a knight garbed in green chain mail and sporting a massive broadsword wreaked havoc among the Dekras invaders. Nearby, a beautiful young woman-knight was displaying skills of equal merit as she dispatched foes with blinding thrusts and swipes of her longsword. Her skillful display did not go overlooked by the burly knight.

"Neatly done for a womanly knight, Jadiane!" he crowed. Jadiane shook her head as though expecting such a comment, then launched an attack on another Dekras foot soldier.

"Why, thank you, Sir Gaurth," she responded somewhat glib as she engaged her next foe. "I'll cherish that."

"But of course any knight should prevail against mere *pons*," Gaurth added with a mischievous smirk.

"Pons are we?" snarled a nearby Dekras foot soldier. "We shall see, sir knight. Your blood will spill the same as ours!" The enemy foot soldier punctuated his bold oath with a fierce swing of his pikestaff, but Gaurth parried easily and slashed the man brutally across the chest.

"Not by your hand – footman," the knight snickered. But even while defenders like Gaurth and Jadiane repelled the onslaught of Dekras soldiers, they could hear the attack on the castle continuing in earnest as Kryzol's minions hurled themselves repeatedly at the high walls and main gates. Still the castle held. For now, fewer attackers were making their way onto the terrace where Gaurth and Jadiane and the other Kathorian defenders fought off the onslaught.

A hunched figure garbed in a hooded robe scurried into the fray, drawing a look of annoyance from Sir Gaurth. It was Druid Lothi, a wiry man of some sixty years but clearly no one to be trifled with, for he flaunted all the bearing of an aged cobra. He wielded a vicious looking scimitar in his left hand and had the air of one who relished using it.

"To the east wall ... quickly," his raspy old voice screeched. "As many as can be spared!"

Gaurth stared at him in bewilderment. Several others did the same. "But here is where the enemy is strongest," the burly knight protested.

"And it's the east wall where we are weakest. Come, I need a good fifty of you there!"

Jadiane and Gaurth looked at one another skeptically, then acquiesced to the druid's authority. Lothi nodded in acknowledgment. With a sweeping gesture of his sword, he signaled a number of other knights and footmen to follow.

On a distant hillock, two druids garbed in the maroon of Dekras conversed with a handsome man, lean and dark; raptor-like. He was draped in a similar cowled robe, silken and far more exquisite. His appearance suggested a graceful fifties, but his pale eyes and cold features indicated one whose years of life contained more time than could be measured. The two druids standing before him — one elderly, the other gaunt and young — addressed him as though speaking with a deity. A band of Dekras knights surrounded the hillock protectively.

"The diversion has been made, yes?" the cowled leader asked of his two subordinates.

"If their traitor's signal is to be trusted, Lord Kryzol," the younger of the two replied. The Druid-King shot him a cross look, causing the man to bow his head.

"It should not be long then before Kieman and Shaikela are taken?" the Druid-King asked quietly, making it clear no answer other than "yes" was acceptable. Both druids nodded.

"They're not to be slain, sire?" responded the younger druid.

"And see Kieman's death rally his minions into greater resistance? No, Druid Suhn. Better to capture and degrade an enemy king than give his grieving subjects cause to fight on."

"And Queen Shaikela ...?" queried the older of the two subordinates, a caution in his tone that caused his voice to quiver.

"The 'Queen' of Kathor is *my* concern, dear Malbric."

The elder druid dipped his head reverently, knowing well no further discussion on the subject would be held.

* * *

Gaurth, Jadiane, and a large contingent of knights and foot soldiers defended the east wall, which did not appear to harbor the same danger as the main gates. Sir Gaurth expressed the skepticism felt by all of them. "This is a waste of our numbers," he growled to anyone in listening range as he glanced about. "And where has Lothi gone to now? I would send some of our men back to –"

An abrupt commotion from the direction of the north quarter of the castle terrace interrupted him. Cries of "Breach. The main gates are breached!" ripped the air. Gaurth and Jadiane both looked at each other. Gaurth shook his head furiously.

A portly middle-aged druid appeared – a man who might have been regarded comically if not for his stately bearing. Gaurth addressed him respectfully. "High Druid Duwin, what is the –"

"The battle is lost," the chunky man replied before Gaurth could even finish. "We are betrayed. Come, we can only flee now!"

Gaurth, Jadiane, and a number of the others stood motionless, hoping they had not heard correctly. Duwin waved his longsword fiercely in response for them to comply. A moment more and they followed.

As the forces of Castle Kathor fled through the rear gates, a swarm of Dekras warriors poured freely over the unguarded battlements and through the breached main gate.

CHAPTER TWO
Abandoned in the Wild

The courtiers and warriors of Kathor were scattered about in a
glade thick with pines. Grouped closely together were King Kieman
and his wife Shaikela — the queen looking utterly drained — while
the two knights, Sir Gaurth and Lady Jadiane, hovered protectively
over both. High Druid Duwin stood in their midst — while another
druid, a middle-aged man, lurked just outside their immediate circle.
Nearby, Turi, a boy of some nineteen years, watched this premier
group studiously. He wore the standard armor of a foot soldier: a
thin leather tunic over his torso, vambraces and greaves on his
forearms and shins, and a leather cap over his head. In spite of his
martial apparel, he bore all the look of a house kitten tossed
outdoors.

"Can there be any doubt it was that wretch Lothi who made that
breach possible?" growled Gaurth. "And where is he now?"

King Kieman's response was a look of melancholy resignation.

Gaurth turned almost accusingly to Duwin and the other druid.

"It's those dark arts you druids practice that fired his treachery!"

"The Cryptic Arts are of great worth when wielded justly, Sir
Gaurth," Duwin countered wearily.

Turi, the boy garbed in foot soldier's armor, harkened uneasily at

Gaurth's last quip.

"Then tell me, High Druid," Gaurth persisted, "why does it then seem —"

"Please!" King Kieman broke in, flustered. He looked utterly spent and it seemed the mail armor he wore all but forced him into a weary crouch, the plain bronze crown on his head appearing every bit as burdensome to him. "Is it not enough that Lothi's treachery has made it so we are scattered here in our own woods like a band of rogues? Quarreling will not help." He lowered his voice to a hush. "And it does the Queen no good to hear this sort of talk."

Several yards away, Shaikela, barely able to sit upright in her horse-drawn wicker cart, strained to hear them as two healers, an older woman and a beautiful teenage girl, attended to her.

Duwin edged closer to Gaurth and spoke confidentially. "It was her cryptic strength that kept Kryzol and his druids at bay. And it has cost her dearly." Duwin cast a sidelong glance at Shaikela who had been listening throughout their debate and overheard most of it. Weakly she raised a hand as though gesturing in assurance she would recover. She turned and, with a wave, dismissed the two healers. She tried sitting up taller.

Kirspen, the younger of the two healers, spied the leather-armored boy and slipped on over to him. She nudged him playfully. Turi tried ignoring her gesture, but she persisted. He frowned and put a finger anxiously to his lips, cautioning her not to speak while the leaders debated their plight. Kirspen eyed him back sharply, making it clear she was more than mindful of the situation.

The king walked quietly over to Gaurth and spoke softly, respectfully to the brash knight. "You have just cause for your anger, Sir Gaurth. If not for that breach in our north gate, the Queen might well have kept the Druid-King's conjurings in check ..."

"And our castle would not be gone, Sire" said Gaurth flatly.

Kieman nodded in sad agreement. "I never thought Lothi would go so far as to ... Oh, I am a fool I suppose."

Kirspen, hearing Lothi's name brought up again, leaned over and whispered in Turi's ear, her long wool cloak seeming to shiver along with her words. "I don't know about you, but I've always been afraid of Druid Lothi."

"A lot of people feel that way about him, Kirspen," Turi whispered back. It was clear he was among them. The two teenagers looked entirely out of place at this impromptu council being held in the woods, where Kathor's vaunted leaders were scattered like a lost flock.

Jadiane, Gaurth, Kieman, and Duwin bunched in closer. "None of us thought Lothi would betray us like that, Sire," Duwin said to Kieman, drawing a smirk and a frown from Gaurth. Kirspen meanwhile nudged Turi again, her face bearing a vixen look that showed she hoped to temper the gravity of the situation.

"Turi," she whispered mischievously, "have you ever noticed old Lothi's nose hairs? They poke out like little grey hooks."

Turi snickered at that in spite of himself, drawing a reproachful look from High Druid Duwin who overheard it. The boy clammed back up and gave the angel-faced Kirspen a mildly stern look of his own that said, 'Now look what you did.' Kirspen shrugged innocently in response.

The middle-aged druid, Mur, hustled over to the king, speaking urgently. "Sire, Kryzol's raiding parties may not be far off."

"So I've heard, Druid Mur," said Kieman, trying to sound calmer than he actually felt. The king's worn, leathern face betrayed the instant fears he harbored. "And I've been told by one of our scouts it is *Rojun Thayne* who leads them."

Duwin and Jadiane both stirred at Kieman's mention of Rojun Thayne. A hush fell over the glade. Turi and Kirspen looked at one another, frightened by the name alone, both suddenly like a pair of children who had just been told the boogey man was at the door.

Gaurth, however, brandished his sword as though readying for an attack right then and there. "Well then, we best prepare for it!"

"Flight would be more prudent now, Sir Gaurth," said Kieman.

"I do not fear this 'dread knight-captain' of Kryzol's," Gaurth retorted.

"And none here thinks you do ... or that Lady Jadiane fears Rojun Thayne either," Kieman said patiently. "But it's wiser that we seek better position now, so we might roust our citizens and strike later with strength. Here, disbanded, we are at the enemy's mercy."

Gaurth looked from Kieman to Duwin, then to Jadiane, who nodded that she agreed with the king. He stared over at the physically spent Shaikela who struggled now just to maintain consciousness.

Turi and Kirspen simply watched wide-eyed. And Turi could not help eying Jadiane, smitten with each step she took, with each spoken word from her that was like harp music to his ears. An annoyed look from Kirspen told Turi he wasn't being discreet enough about any of it. He turned his attention back in the direction of Duwin.

"We must move quickly then, Sire," said the high druid.

Jadiane walked over to join Kieman and Duwin. She bore the elegant, supple look of a natural athlete, carrying herself with more of a courtly dignity than that of a soldier. Turi let his eyes follow each of her steps, trying to be more subtle but not succeeding. Kirspen noticed and rolled her eyes, frowning to herself.

"What is it you require of us then, My King?" Lady Jadiane asked quietly. She overheard Gaurth snicker none too softly to a nearby male knight ...

"Only in Kathor are maidens permitted to take up manly arms and act as knights." Gaurth's fellow knight snickered back at the quip and Duwin scowled at them both as though reprimanding children.

Turi and Kirspen also heard the exchange between the two knights and stared at one another, surprised by Sir Gaurth's cavalier humor right in front of the king himself — who did not appear amused. Kieman gave Gaurth a hard look before addressing everyone again.

"There is a way we might outmaneuver Kryzol," said King Kieman. "He will be expecting a retreat to our strongest hamlet — Gruton."

"And rightly so. There's little else we can do, Sire," agreed Duwin.

"Then we best make way," said Gaurth.

"Ah, but we shall fool them instead," quipped Kieman. Everyone stared at him, perplexed. The king smiled wryly. "The enemy will expect a large force to escort the Queen and me through the woods." The group nodded in agreement. "And a large force will indeed make its way toward Gruton — before turning east to Nuwich."

"Nuwich?" snapped Gaurth. Kieman nodded smugly. Most had reacted as Sir Gaurth. Turi especially flinched at the mention of Nuwich.

"Queen Shaikela and I will leave now, but with a much smaller party, one that is difficult to detect. We will go directly to Nuwich.

But the rest will draw the attention of Sir Rojun and his roving pack by first making toward Gruton."

They all continued staring at him incredulously. Kieman merely smiled again at everyone's bewilderment. "Now, as for those who shall accompany me ..." He motioned toward Druid Mur and a nearby knight and several foot soldiers, then walked gingerly toward Turi and Kirspen who both appeared stunned.

"Is such a move safe?" Jadiane asked, sounding every bit as skeptical as Gaurth.

"Is any move safe in a game of this sort?" the king responded wryly, mustering together the ones he had chosen to accompany his party. "You, Lady Jadiane, shall command those who escort Queen Shaikela and me to Nuwich."

Gaurth looked flabbergasted by that, though not nearly so as Jadiane herself. Duwin just smiled, pleased by the king's choice. And hearing it, Turi now beamed with pride. "And what shall your strongest warriors do while you make for that bumpkin village?" quipped Gaurth, clearly miffed by the king's unexpected selection. "Without enough knights to guard you, those footmen ... those pons will serve as little more than battle fodder."

Kieman eyed him crossly, not failing to notice how Turi and the entire escort party were stung by Gaurth's blatant insult. The king drew himself up. "It is the High Druid and you, Sir Gaurth, who shall distract Rojun Thayne and draw him toward Gruton where he expects me to go. And it may likely be you who contends with Thayne before we reunite in Nuwich. If you fail, there will be no cause to fortify or send riders to roust our villages. We will all be captured or dead."

CHAPTER THREE
The Cryptic Sense

Kryzol stood peering out the open window of his castle chambers which were decorated with exquisite tapestries and furniture. His frosty eyes roamed the horizon then turned back inside. Books, scrolls, vials and other mystical paraphernalia filled most of the room. The Druid-King took a long impatient breath, then turned his gaze back out at the southern horizon. He glared evilly in that direction as he recalled the events of earlier in the day. In spite of his carefully wrought scheme, the crème of Kathor had escaped him ... in particular his traitorous cousin Shaikela.

In response he had sent out his elite commander, Rojun Thayne, a beast of a knight who dealt with foes as easily as most folk swatted pesky gnats. And those who followed Thayne – whose face was always hid behind a great visor – followed him out of the same fear that commanded their allegiance to Kryzol. No, Thayne would not fail, Kryzol thought coldly. And that thought comforted him.

* * *

Out in the Southland woods, a procession of mounted knights garbed in the bright maroon of Dekras galloped along the trail, eyes alert for telltale signs. Directly behind the knights followed a large band of Dekras foot soldiers – pons armed with pikes, halberds and spears. Some hacked at the surrounding thickets while others scampered off into the trees and searched the brush.

And at the head of this huge raiding party, Rojun Thayne rode brazenly atop his war horse. Decked out in his black and maroon plate armor, close-helmed as always, Thayne commanded a figure of terrifying menace. It was said his foes often surrendered without offering a fight, rather than face the "plated demon on horseback." One had only to behold Rojun Thayne here in all his malevolent splendor to recognize this was not folklore, but the accounts of those who had witnessed the Dekras knight-captain in action. The raiding party forged on, supremely confident and readied for victims or opponents, knowing there was no distinction when Thayne led them.

* * *

Elsewhere in the woods, the royal party of Kathorians made their way cautiously along a narrow path through the woods. Druid Mur rode on horseback leading them; he was followed by King Kieman, also riding, and flanked closely by four mounted knights. One of two horse-drawn wicker carts bore the queen's healers – Kirspen and the senior healer. A group of some ten foot soldiers trailed the carts.

Turi rode in the queen's cart, nervous, for he was having a private audience with Queen Shaikela herself. She spoke hoarsely and with great effort and it made him all the more uncomfortable as he felt it only contributed to her condition. She tugged her long robe of silver-and-green fleece more tightly around her, shivering a bit.

"Turi, do you know why you've been chosen to go with the Royal Party?" She seemed almost maternal in her regard for him, though clearly not old enough to be his mother. Indeed, her slender features and smooth bronze skin gave her the deceptive look of one not long out of her teens. Turi caught from the corner of one eye, a glimpse of Lady Jadiane riding alongside the cart (out of earshot) and, even here and now, could not help being distracted by her. It actually helped him feel less uneasy in the queen's presence. And in spite of her condition and the gravity of their situation, Shaikela picked up on the boy's distraction and smiled inwardly to herself.

"My Lady, isn't it my duty to serve when danger lurks ... though I am only a pon?"

"You are one of the High Druid's acolytes," she corrected him. He lowered his head, feeling mildly rebuked.

"But now I've been ordered to take up arms. I've never been good at that sort of thing. These other fellows here, they're true foot soldiers and ... "

Shaikela waved him silent with a brush of her hand. "My needs are beyond what a soldier has to offer," she said softly. He eyed her curiously, feeling all the more out of sorts. Shaikela leaned in closer. "You are a born master of the Cryptic Sense, Turi."

Had it not been the Queen herself, Turi might have laughed at that. Instead he shook inwardly, feeling a flicker of disquiet.

"Queen Shaikela, I've been taught nothing more than the basic order of nature. Duwin has shown me little in the high science of –"

"Your conjuring strength in the ways of soil and water ... of fire and wind ... is far more *active* than you know." She paused a moment to catch her breath, brushing her raven black hair away from her face. Turi again felt guilty over the way she struggled on his behalf. "Duwin told me of you months ago, Turi. Do you recall the day I came to your classes at the Academy Building?"

Turi remembered all too well the day Queen Shaikela had visited Duwin's classes when the rest of the high druid's acolytes were present. Every one of them had been enormously distracted by the presence of the beautiful young queen and had feared making fools of themselves. But when she and Duwin had taken special note of Turi performing a classroom conjuring exercise, it was a moment the young acolyte would never forget. He had been called upon to demonstrate, before the queen, his recently learned telekinetic command over a pan of water where he caused "minor waves" to break inside it.

"The High Druid said you might one day hold great command over the Living Energy that governs all of our elements ... a match even for my own, perhaps."

Turi gaped at her in disbelief. "That could never be!"

Shaikela nodded softly, affirming it could indeed.

"But Duwin has said nothing of this to me."

"Because it was not yet time," she countered. "There is much more to study before you are ready to serve among the Order of Druids." She paused and drew a long breath, tiring more. "But time is no longer our ally."

Turi stared at her, unable to respond. The long line of trees and shrubs and low cliffs rolled by as the small procession pressed on. Turi realized the queen was fading fast but did not dare reach over to aid her. He glanced round, hoping to catch the attention of Kirspen or the senior healer, but Shaikela waved her hand that she was all right and able to continue.

"You have heard Duwin speak of the Power Roots?"

Turi hesitated a moment, unsure where she might be headed with this, then recited as though in class: "The greatest conductors of the Living Energy, yes."

With a tremendous effort, Shaikela unsheathed from within her robes, a long silvery dirk which glowed as though afire, the very one she had wielded during the battle with Kryzol's forces. Turi gasped. She held up a finger in a hushing gesture.

"*The Silver Blade* ..." His voice dropped to a hoarse whisper. "The High Druid spoke of it once."

She nodded. "For each druid, the shape of the Root is different. When the day comes, you will shape and wield your own Root of Power."

Turi eyed her almost suspiciously. "My Lady, why show this to me?"

Shaikela summoned the last of her waning strength. "If anything ill comes of me, Turi, this must never fall into Kryzol's hands."

Turi stared at her, utterly perplexed.

"And he will come for it," she added solemnly.

He held her penetrating gaze as long as he could sustain it, then looked down. "I ... will make sure, My Lady."

Shaikela smiled softly, relief on her tired young face.

"Very good. And Turi — you are not a 'Nuwich bumpkin,' nor a 'mere pon.'"

Turi swallowed quietly. He wanted dearly to reach over and touch her arm in thanks, but restrained himself.

"I must rest now, Turi. Please tell Kirspen to come here. She knows what to do for me." She smiled weakly, her light brown eyes straining to focus. "You like dear Kirspen ... yes?"

Turi nodded, pleased to see that this comforted her.

"See that the Blade is wielded well," she whispered softly, firmly, before fading into unconsciousness.

CHAPTER FOUR

Plots

—

Gaurth and Duwin rode at the head of the ragtag procession of Kathorian soldiers, their hushed voices and the quiet tromp of horse hooves and booted feet over the leafy ground signaling the group's progress through the narrow woodland path.

"But not all from Dekras are as foul as you think, Sir Gaurth," Duwin protested. "Simply because their ways seem mysterious and —"

"Secretive. Secretive and filled with sorcery," Gaurth interrupted.

"Science, Sir Gaurth ... science."

Gaurth eyed him skeptically.

"And it doesn't make them evil," Duwin continued. "Any more than our own Queen is evil."

Gaurth frowned, not liking the High Druid's making his point in that way. "Queen Shaikela is different," the burly knight countered. "She abandoned the ways of her Dekras Cult willingly."

"Thus she is good and those who remain in Dekras are all bad?" Duwin replied facetiously.

"If they choose to stay there under Kryzol's rule, yes."

"Ah, Sir Gaurth, I do not know how I endure logic such as yours. Doesn't it seem that the folk of Dekras might regard us with suspicion too? That there may be cause for people who have dwelled there for so long to be wary of strangers – especially those who dared settle on the very borders of the Old Tundra?"

Several nearby foot soldiers and knights, eavesdropping on the two, exchanged glances, well accustomed to such debates between them.

"Pah! That was nearly a hundred years ago and, and ..."

"And they watched those numbers grow," Duwin added smoothly.

"It wasn't our Southern Clans who began all this conjuring of Dark Arts, Duwin!"

"Nor was that practiced in Dekras until Kryzol began it."

Gaurth's frown deepened.

"And not all druids practice such things, Sir Gaurth. The use of the Cryptic Sense isn't evil in itself. No more than is the use of swords." They passed along a rocky mount. Gaurth stared up at it suspiciously, ever wary of an ambush.

"Gaurth, have you never wondered why Kathor is blessed with such fair weather ... or why our woodlands are so lush?"

"That is not the same," Gaurth snapped, his gaze shifting back toward the druid. Your ways with gardens and trees and the like is well known, Duwin."

Duwin eyed him back flatly. "It is our Queen – Shaikela of Dekras – who commands the elements thus, Sir Gaurth."

Gaurth pursed his lips, knowing he had no argument for that.

"Well, I've always had great respect for the Lady Shaikela. But do not expect me to regard others of that race in the same way."

They approached a glen where the small force slowed, preparing for a temporary halt. Duwin held Gaurth's gaze.

"Then while you condemn the rest of Shaikela's race," the druid added smoothly, "do remember there were Southerners like our own Lothi who also came here to settle on the borders of the Old Tundra."

* * *

Kryzol, garbed in his usual exquisite robes, eyed the two druids who had been with him during the siege of Castle Kathor. The older of the two, Malbric, appeared especially ill at ease.

"He is here, My Lord," the elder druid said with an air that hinted of resignation and disapproval. Kryzol nodded for the man to admit the visitor. The older druid walked over to the arched doorway and gestured in Lothi who was flanked by two Dekras knights.

Kryzol regarded Lothi a moment, then motioned to his own two druids, indicating that they and the knights should all leave. While exiting, both druids eyed Lothi with blatant suspicion.

"We shall be waiting nearby, Lord Kryzol," spoke the younger.

"Understood Suhn," Kryzol replied, mildly amused.

Lothi watched Kryzol's henchmen leave then turned to him.

"Your underlings doubt me, Sire," the elder from Kathor said, his gaze and his voice both hollow.

"Druid Suhn is young," crooned the druid-king of Dekras. "And Malbric is quite set in his ways. He dislikes any who hail from the hated Southlands."

Lothi bristled nervously. "Have I not proven my worth?" he asked, his dust grey eyes nearly pleading.

"To Dekras — or to yourself, Druid Lothi?"

Lothi contained a subtle sneer. "I am not without ambition, Lord Kryzol. It would be a lie to say I've not been soured by Kieman's choosing that dolt Duwin as his High Druid. The man is nothing more than a tinkering alchemist."

"It was nearly ten years ago that Kieman passed you over in favor of Duwin. It seems you are a patient fellow."

"There was no opportunity till now, Lord Kryzol."

"Indeed. My own High Druid is dead but a month...and one of Kieman's very own seeks to replace him."

"Or continue serving under Duwin who wasted those years merely dabbling in the Arts... he and his bumbling acolytes," Lothi murmured, glowering from beneath his wrinkled brow. "While I sought to strengthen myself."

"Then should I not see you as a threat?" Kryzol said, taking a step toward Lothi who eyed him back with a wry, cautious smile.

"You are a direct one, My Lord," he uttered lightly. Kryzol laughed politely and Lothi frowned, not sure what to make of it. "Your work in the Dark Arts has taken you far beyond what any druid has ever dreamed, Sire. Fools like Duwin cannot comprehend such journeys!"

"'Fools' like Duwin convinced Kieman that my practice was too dangerous to share," Kryzol countered.

Lothi shifted defensively. "I disagreed with Duwin."

"Mmm, so you did. But it was that tinkering alchemist who had your King's ear," Kryzol seethed, a pang of irritation showing now in the pale blue eyes that contained something of a reptile's glare. "If not, druids from all of the provinces and kingdoms would have united here to explore the untapped might of the elements!" The druid-king stiffened abruptly, as though embarrassed by his own outburst. "But for Kieman and Duwin," he added quietly, his tone more controlled. He smiled thinly at Lothi with an air of reassurance. "Of course, I know you did all you could, Lothi. And had my dear cousin Shaikela done the same and brought that sweet-tongued King of yours underfoot, as instructed, Kathor might have been contained more ... peaceably."

Lothi spoke cautiously. "How strong is the Queen of Kathor?"

Kryzol drew a long, uncomfortable breath. "So long as she holds the Silver Blade...none of us might stand against her." His narrow mouth rippled as he grimaced with that acknowledgment. "If not for your aid, Druid Lothi, we might never have taken that castle."

Lothi breathed a quiet sigh of relief, pleased at last with the recognition he had so dearly sought. He bowed his cowled head, concealing a tiny curl of a smile he strained to withhold.

"So...you would see the fall of Kathor then?" Kryzol asked.

Lothi raised his weathered head and nodded slowly, firmly as the druid-king's eyes bore into his, searching perhaps for signs of doubt. Lothi stared back at him just as firmly and offered a wolfish little grin, reassuring his commitment.

"High Druid of Dekras you shall be then," Kryzol said smoothly.

Lothi nodded, trembling with satisfaction.

"But a most important gesture of loyalty is required of you now, my High Druid," Kryzol added softly. "One that will aid us in containing Shaikela."

Lothi looked at him, puzzled, his ridged brow furrowing.

"It is no less than I required of Malbric and Suhn." The druid-king paused then stretched out his hand. "Your Power Root, Druid Lothi."

Lothi gaped, nearly paralyzed with shock. Kryzol nodded as though in answer to the unspoken question. There would be no discussion on the matter. With a monumental effort, Lothi reached into the folds of his robes and withdrew a black cone-shaped object that glowed with a cold light. Painfully he handed it over to Kryzol, then seemed to shrivel and diminish in size no sooner than the black cone left his hand.

"It is a small sacrifice — until we have harnessed my cousin," Kryzol added glibly.

Lothi shook his head absently, a man now unsure of his part of the bargain. He was numb, barely able to muster the desperate words that came from his mouth. "But even if we do subdue the Queen, the remnants of Kathor's army still go unchecked. If they rally their village militias ..."

"Sir Rojun attends to that even now," Kryzol reassured him, then turned and strode off, leaving Lothi by himself to ponder his own actions and the fate he had chosen of his own accord.

CHAPTER FIVE
Ambush!

A temporary encampment had been set up. Turi sat quietly on a cracked oak stump, tapping his sheathed sword absently and staring moonstruck at Jadiane across the camp as she conferred with Shaikela. His mind wandered to places private and dreamy.

"Can't take your eyes off of her, can you?" a voice quipped from behind him. Startled, he turned to see Kirspen standing there. Turi flushed with embarrassment.

"Eh ... no," he stammered. "I mean, that is, the Queen still seems very weak."

"The Queen ... ?" Kirspen replied glibly.

Turi did not fail to recognize the implication in her tone. "Well, yes, Kirspen. You saw for yourself today. But you, eh, realize I cannot tell you what we spoke of earlier," he added, affecting an air of mystery. Kirspen frowned, not taken in by it.

"Why, of course. And I think it's right and proper that you stand here now and watch Lady Jadiane speak with her, Turi."

Turi stared at her, perplexed by her tone and too embarrassed to recognize the hint of jealousy the young healer failed to contain.

"Well the King did choose Lady Jadiane as Chief Guard of the Royal Party." His gaze drifted over to Jadiane as he spoke. "Did you know that in Narek where Lady Jadiane is from, she was a swords master? She was the only woman to match up against the men back there. And she's the only woman –"

"– to ever become a knight of Kathor," Kirspen broke in, a tinge of impatience in her voice. "Turi, do you honestly think there's anyone from Kathor who doesn't know that story by now?"

"Oh, I'm sure you're right, Kirspen. But it's all just so remarkable. Why, just a month ago while escorting some courtiers to Gruton, she battled off an ambush of road bandits who –"

"Yes I know. The senior healer and I tended to the courtiers and soldiers who were hurt in that attack. There's something to be said for healing people as well as hurting them," she added curtly.

Turi stared at her, aware suddenly he may have offended her. "Kirspen, I know that. Being apprentice to the senior healer is very noble. But I just –"

" – admire Lady Jadiane."

"People all over Kathor do. Ever since she came here –"

" – six years ago. That would have made her about nineteen, Turi. Your age ... back then."

Turi frowned, not pleased at being reminded of this age disparity. His gaze shifted back to Jadiane and King Kieman conferring as they assisted the queen. "Ah, but the likes of Lady Jadiane remain young forever."

Kirspen rolled her eyes and shook her head. She moved to change the subject. "And how does serving as a soldier suit you?"

Turi glanced down in embarrassment at the short sword sheathed at his hip. "Sir Gaurth is right, Kirspen. Pons serve as little more than battle fodder."

A cross look flashed over Kirspen's face, her chestnut eyes showing a glint of annoyance. "That's not so, Turi. None of those knights have the right to call any soldier a pon."

Turi walked over and put a hand to Kirspen's shoulder, as one would do with a good friend. He smiled sadly. "Kirspen, the only reason I even have this sword is because so many of our warriors were killed in the attack."

"So? You are the High Druid's prize pupil! I've heard him say as much when he was speaking with the King and Queen."

"And I've overheard Lothi say to them that 'Duwin makes far too great a fuss over that precocious brat.'"

"Lothi is a jealous, wretched old man!" Kirspen snapped back, a shiver yet zipping through her body at the mere mention of the elder druid. "And his thoughts are very dirty."

"Does he really look at you like ...?"

"It doesn't matter. He's gone now."

Turi drew himself up protectively, eying the angel-faced young beauty now as though he were a knight assigned to guard her.

"Well if it ever does happen again ..."

Kirspen touched him affectionately on the arm, flattered. "You sound like Sir Gaurth now."

Turi laughed skeptically. "Sir Gaurth surely doesn't think much of me."

"Oh, Turi ... Sir Gaurth is so much wind," she giggled. "I don't think he means half of what he says when he puffs up the way he does." She kept her hand on his arm, the gesture affecting him strangely. Turi looked into her eyes, seeing something there he didn't fully understand. Kirspen stared back at him dreamily.

"Kirspen, I ..."

He groped for the next words but could not make them out clearly enough in his head. Kirspen felt suddenly just as awkward and she moved to change the subject. "Turi, would you show me what Duwin taught you about that difficult conjuring? The Sprinkling. Didn't he say water was your strongest element?"

Turi looked relieved with the distraction. "Well it's really not all that difficult."

Kirspen pointed toward a nearby tree. "See the apple tree over by that patch of rampion? Please try?" Turi rose reluctantly and stared over at some trees near the edge of the glade, all bearing small green apples. He and Kirspen walked toward them — under the watchful eyes of a pair of camp guards. He was unable to resist another glance back at Lady Jadiane who happened to be looking in his direction at the moment. Jadiane recognized the nature of his stare and could not help smiling at his boyish innocence. Turi fairly melted as he caught her look, interpreting it otherwise.

None of this escaped Kirspen's eye and she drew him smoothly over to a clump of brush where she tugged up a handful of rampion and offered him some of the edible roots. Turi nodded awkwardly in acknowledgment, then concentrated on the task at hand.

The nearby foot soldiers watched curiously as Turi's eyes closed into slits and he began making small passes in the air with his hands, while murmuring softly. His eyes popped open suddenly and his focus locked onto a twisted tree limb bearing several apples. On the outer skin of two apples, tiny rents appeared faintly, then deepened into fissures which sprang forth with small sprinkling streams of juice that spurted freely into the air. Turi stepped back and he and Kirspen exchanged a glance, giggling. They scooted closer to the tree and opened their mouths to catch the sweet juices spilling forth. The two guards, meantime, exchanged looks of astonishment that bordered on superstitious awe.

Turi and Kirspen both noticed the looks on the guards' faces and could not suppress mischievous smirks slipping over their own faces. Kirspen seized the opportunity to reach over and carefully slide a hand into Turi's. He did not seem to mind one bit, even seeming comfortable with the gesture – but then dropped her hand abruptly.

Turi stared steadfastly into a thicket behind the apple tree.

And lurking within that thicket, a face, swarthy and sullen – the head fairly covered by a leather helm of bright maroon – stared back. Before Turi could even react to the sudden appearance of this intruder, an ugly yell broke the bright afternoon air and a flood of Dekras warriors poured out from the surrounding trees! Turi heard Kirspen call out his name, but the two were separated instantly as he was bowled over during the initial onslaught.

Pandemonium struck the camp as the royal party of Kathor was taken completely unawares by the ambush. The Kathorian knights recovered quickly though and rallied, their swordsmanship clearly of a skill that was too much for the charging enemy foot soldiers. Strength of numbers, however, was against the Kathorians and they were soon pressed back.

Lady Jadiane stood protectively by Queen Shaikela, striking this way and that and uttering the battle oaths of her home village as she called out commands in an attempt to rally her bewildered charges. And close by, King Kieman displayed his own skill with the blade as he dispatched enemy warriors from a group that tried attacking strategically between himself and where Jadiane battled by the queen's cart.

Turi still lay on the ground. He looked up to see Jadiane fighting off a crunch of foot soldiers; then he glanced about anxiously. "Kirspen ..." he whispered to himself. He spotted her mixed in with a group of courtiers being shielded by some soldiers. Though greatly outnumbered, the Kathorians were more than holding their own. And then came the thunder of hooves and the din of men on horseback. And above that din rose the cold laughter of one whose booming voice dominated the entire glade.

Still pressed to the ground, Turi rolled toward a nearby clump of bushes and tall weeds, none too soon. Bursting out from the now widened woodland trail came the knight-captain of Dekras – Rojun Thayne himself. He was flanked by several other mounted knights, all garbed in maroon chain-mail armor. Turi shuddered, transfixed by the sight of Rojun Thayne who seemed more of a spectre in his glittering plate armor and closed helm. The hiss of Thayne's great morning star weapon, the spiked ball twirling round-and-round overhead, compelled Turi to remain in the safety of his weedy haven.

Thayne's explosive emergence onto the scene rallied the Dekras forces, while the Kathorians were instantly demoralized by the dread knight of lore charging into the heat of the fray and batting away would-be attackers as a huge bear might bat away so many dogs.

Thayne made a direct line for the king and queen. A Kathorian knight tried engaging him and Thayne walloped him brutally with a swipe of the morning star! The man fell dead from his horse.

Turi stared in horror, while Kirspen watched from across the glade, terrified by the brutish Thayne. The Dekras knight-captain swiftly positioned himself between the wicker cart where Shaikela struggled just to sit upright and where Kieman battled fiercely against a wall of several foot-soldiers.

Nearby, Lady Jadiane paused in her own assault – frozen as she beheld the notorious Rojun Thayne readying himself for a move either at the king or the queen. But a maneuver by some Kathorian foot soldiers who had guessed his strategy distracted him. Thayne turned to meet their attack. King Kieman noticed Thayne momentarily distracted by the soldiers and mowed right through two Dekras warriors in his path. Boldly he urged his horse straight toward the huge knight-captain. But he found himself blocked by one of his own men, the middle-aged druid, Mur, who guided his own mount into the king's path.

"No, My Lord," cried Druid Mur. "He will kill you!"

"We shall see about that!" shouted Kieman. Mur shook his head "no" in vehement protest.

"You can do nothing here now!" the druid cried. With that, Mur pulled out a small staff from within his robes. "Flee ... I beg you, Sire!"

"I cannot," the stately king replied.

Mur grimaced in response. "Then forgive me, King." The druid then waved his staff, chanting a few incoherent words. A tiny cloud of dust formed out of thin air, knit instantly into a ball, then whipped fiercely into the flank of Kieman's horse. The druid hissed eerily and the king's mount squealed and bolted away — Kieman no longer able to command it. Mur hollered to the group of courtiers and soldiers with Kirspen. "Fly with him! Go, protect the King!"

Two knights with the group nodded urgently and began a hasty retreat while Thayne was still occupied by the foot soldiers. One of Kieman's knights yanked Kirspen onto the back of his horse, urging the rest to flee on other horses, in the carts, or to simply run. Kirspen screamed frantically for Turi, but he was crouched in the brush across the glade, too frightened to creep out into the open. Several Kathorian soldiers helped a courtier onto a knight's horse, while some clambered into a cart; the rest followed on foot. In all the confusion they escaped — while Turi watched from his cover.

"Kirspen ..." he whispered to himself as he watched the small group disappear into the thick of the trees.

Kieman's druid turned his attention to Queen Shaikela who had struggled to her feet, trying vainly to muster a conjuring, while the senior healer gestured to the cart driver to make haste with the horses.

Having dispatched the intrepid band of footmen, Thayne glanced around, surveying the battle — and spotted his primary prey fleeing. He fairly snarled and veered his horse after them.

Lady Jadiane caught Thayne's action and moved to intercept. So did Druid Mur. Jadiane saw the druid make his move. "No ... Mur, no! I'll take him!"

Rojun Thayne laughed from inside his steel helm. He met the

druid's charge with a hissing swipe of the morning star. The spiked ball caught the druid square on the cheek with a resounding crack — decapitating him so the man's horse momentarily hosted a robed, headless rider.

Watching from his cover in the brush, Turi's stomach heaved as he retched out his innards. Rojun Thayne, meanwhile, saw only Lady Jadiane barring his path now to the queen. He drove his huge war steed toward the wicker cart. "Stand aside — woman! Else you'll suffer the same as your druid!" Thayne yelled. Jadiane regarded the brutish knight-captain fearfully, but defiantly.

"You'll not lay your hands on your betters — scum of Dekras!" she hollered. Thayne laughed once more. Turi peered up at the sound of Jadiane's cry and watched, mesmerized. He barely noticed that the courtiers guiding the queen's wicker cart had finally got it moving. It was heading in his very direction. At the same time, Jadiane and Thayne met head on.

The battle between Rojun Thayne and Jadiane was short-lived.

With a single swipe of the morning star, Thayne walloped Jadiane hard in the chest and knocked her senseless from her horse! She did not stir from the spot where she landed and appeared dead. Turi looked on tearfully, in total disbelief, as he remained crouched in the thorny brush. "No!" he cried out involuntarily, his voice lost in the din.

"Farewell Lady Knight," Rojun Thayne crowed. "'Twas ungallant of me to slay one so feeble!"

Turi buried his face in his hands, but was diverted instantly from his grief by the clatter of the wicker cart as it passed the thicket. He glanced up. Queen Shaikela was peering straight through the bushes and into his eyes. She reached wearily into the folds of her robes and withdrew the silvery dagger she had shown him earlier. The queen nodded to him knowingly, then tossed the blade deep into the thicket. The cart rambled on past Turi's hideaway. Turi pressed himself flat to the ground as Thayne and his men overtook the fleeing cart a moment later and finished off its remaining defenders. The senior healer was among those slain.

Turi crouched low, his knees and hands cut by the briars and thorns as he listened to the horrid commotion in the glade. He glanced off into the depths of the thicket where Shaikela had tossed the Silver Blade, waited a long moment, then crawled off in that direction.

* * *

The clamor behind Turi faded away as he scrambled awkwardly through the undergrowth, the mossy forest smells filling his nostrils and lungs. The tears that had spilled down his face earlier had seeped through his lips and he heaved and gasped open-mouthed at their thick salty taste. His disbelieving mind refused to absorb entirely the horrors he had beheld this day and now ...

A soft thrumming broke into his thoughts. He froze, wondering what new deviltry was now thrust upon him. It was close by. He harkened at the sound then turned to veer away from it, but it thrummed more pointedly, as though beckoning him. Turi held still, feeling an odd sensation of warmth that urged him on. He crawled in the direction of this seeming call, as if guided by instinct.

A moment more and he saw the glittering artifact lying near the bole of a tree, thrumming in what seemed almost a greeting. Turi eyed the object cautiously, then finally reached down and gripped hold of the Silver Blade. He bristled as a surge passed through his entire body. He stared at the queen's power root in wonder.

'If anything ill comes of me, this must never fall into Kryzol's hands,' his mind reminded him of her final words. And in the far distance he also still heard, faintly, the voices of the Dekras raiding party. He rose halfway and scrambled off deeper into the woods, the sounds of the ambush finally fading away completely.

Lady Jadiane stirred and rose painfully. She gazed round at the carnage, the sight of it aching her every bit as much as the harsh throbbing in her chest. She groaned in response to the defeat and despair that hurt far worse than the blow Rojun Thayne had dealt her. A friendly snort from nearby distracted her and she turned to see her horse approaching her, the loyal beast having stayed close by the entire time she was out. Jadiane limped toward it, a faint smile on her face that lasted but a moment.

* * *

Turi cringed inside a thicket, shivering from the nightly chill. His eyes darted everywhere at the sounds of insects, owls, and the crackle and crunch of other nocturnal creatures. His hand slid to the handle of the Silver Blade, sheathed and tucked inside his belt, and concealed by his leather tunic. The blade pulsed quietly and he drew back his hand as though stung. He tried closing his eyes to sleep but the many nightly noises prevented it. Turi curled into a ball and hugged himself round the knees more tightly. There would be no comfort or assurance from harm this night or on any to follow.

CHAPTER SIX
Seeking the Blade

Kryzol's private chambers conveyed grimly the subterraneous nature of his yearnings and tastes: the room was stacked with books, scrolls, twisted plants, mystical tapestries, animal skeletons, vials of milky liquids ... the telltale lair of one who basked in practices deemed sorcerous and dark by most folk. And the sweet, pungent odor wafting through the misty chambers confirmed that experiments of a tainted, alternative cut took place in there.

Now the Druid-King hovered over his two underlings, Malbric and Suhn. Both lesser druids were hunched and uneasy, guarded.

"I want the woodland scoured for that Dagger," Kryzol seethed from between his narrow teeth. Suhn bowed his head in supplication.

"Yes, My Lord. But it's been two full days now. It's likely been lost or destroyed. We doubt anyone survived Thayne's ambush."

Kryzol stared silently at Suhn then at Malbric, as a snake might eye a pair of mice. Both fairly melted.

"It appears someone has survived, Druid Suhn. One who may now hold the Silver Blade."

"Yes, My Lord," Suhn responded, knowing there was no other way the matter was to be considered.

"Now find whoever it is," Kryzol said, his voice implying a silent strain for control. "So long as Kieman roams free, or Shaikela's Root of Power lies among that rabble, Kathor remains ever a threat."

"Rojun Thayne leads a large force in search of their king now, Sire," Malbric said in as polite and unassuming a tone he could muster. "But that forest is vast."

"Yes," added Suhn. "Thayne will need more men to assist him in his search. If the traitor Lothi could spare –"

Kryzol eyed Suhn sharply at his use of "traitor."

"That is, if our new ... high druid were to spare some of the men he sent out searching for the Blade ...?" The younger druid paused, uncertain how the druid-king was reading him. "We're merely concerned, Sire, that Kieman might slip away to whichever village he –"

Kryzol silenced him with a wave of his hand, weighing the younger man's words. "I will speak with the High Druid now. Both of you may tend to the needs of our prisoner. I want her fully prepared for the work I have in mind."

Both druids shivered at the notion of what that work might be. They bowed with a show of proper deference and left. Kryzol watched after them, then sat and turned back to his private thoughts.

CHAPTER SEVEN
Nightly Fears

Dusk fell on an unkempt, frightened Turi as he strained to conjure another sprinkling from a tree laden with ripened peaches. The batch he sought hung just out of his reach. He had already dined ravenously on some of the lower hanging fruits, barely taking the time to savor their sweet juices while trying to satiate his hunger. Now he concentrated on the higher ones and finally drew forth a sprinkling from within the branches and twigs to further quench his relentless thirst. Turi ate and drank furtively as he glanced about like a stray cat wary of those who might try snatching away his meager meal. He finished in a rush, then nooked himself away in an earthy burrow near the bole of an oak tree. Not willing to close his eyes and rest yet, he nibbled at some rampion roots he had gathered, glancing this way and that every time he heard a crack or pop of twigs and leaves. Turi shook his head sadly at his plight, then turned and saw he was not alone.

Barely ten-feet from his earthy hideaway, a pair of luminous eyes peered out from a patch of brambles — measuring him with the unmistakable gaze of the predator. Turi all but gagged as the intruder emerged slowly from the brush: a huge wildcat. Its eyes were filled with a feral intelligence that was frightening here in the beast's own element.

Turi groaned silently to himself. His hand slid down and grazed the handle of the Silver Blade, then slid away just as quickly. It settled instead on the pommel of his short sword. The eyes of the bobcat regarded him more intensely. Turi found he could not hold the animal's wild gaze and looked down deliberately. His hand slid away from the sword and he backed farther into the corner of the burrow so his back was now pressed flat against it ... leaving a wider, more vacant area. The wildcat regarded him with a lesser menace now.

Turi concentrated fiercely on the area he had just vacated, straining to suppress a nervous breath that begged to escape his lungs. Some of the dirt, mere feet in front of him, began spinning slowly, picking up gradually in tempo. The wildcat eyed it all cautiously, a low growl emitting from its throat. Turi tensed at that and concentrated more fiercely; the dirt spun more rapidly, forcing a larger groove in the burrow. Then the spinning stopped abruptly. Turi ceased in his conjuring and held perfectly still.

The wildcat regarded the widened groove with a tinge of suspicion. It eyed Turi more curiously, then let out an almost questioning whine. Turi felt a sliver of a smile form on his lips, but didn't budge. Shooting Turi a token warning look, the wildcat slipped, belly flat, into the groove, giving another wary glance toward the human with which it would apparently share its burrow. The cat curled up then closed its eyes, seemingly settling into this odd sleeping arrangement. Turi breathed out a long sigh of relief and, assuming the bobcat was drifting off to sleep, did exactly the same.

CHAPTER EIGHT
Chinook!

In the northern village of Narek, a tiny hamlet built on the rim of a desert that stretched out to a distant mountain cropping, activity was just starting to bustle as it usually did in the morning hours. Two rows of humble, thatched buildings lined a narrow dirt street where vendors and peddlers were starting to set up their stands. A small crowd of simply dressed peasant folk were already out and about, inspecting the displays of fresh vegetables and fruits and wares of crockery and soft muslin clothing.

None, for the moment, took note of the dark speck that had appeared almost magically on the horizon at the foot of the distant mountains. They'd had no cause to gaze out that way, else they would have beheld the frightening speed at which the speck grew and took the shape of a swirling funnel of gusty winds and debris. Not until the screech and howl of those winds first wafted through the air did a few of them peer outward and see the approaching tornado.

Loud gasps and horrified cries of "Chinook" alerted the rest of the milling crowd! Within seconds the village fell into a panic as the tornado drew closer, bearing an eerie, unnatural look. Those close enough to behold the screeching funnel, as it bore down on the doomed village, would later speak of "a pair of ghostly eyes" peering out from what appeared to be a feminine face embedded within the vortex. The roar of the tornado and the cries rising from the village blended together as the filthy spinning cloud descended.

CHAPTER NINE
Stalked!

Turi sat on a rock, chewing on some chestnuts he had gathered off the ground after rising and noting that his feline companion had apparently woken earlier and left without so much as a perfunctory sniff. Or perhaps the big bobcat had hovered over his prone sleeping form before determining he would not have made a fitting meal. Turi shuddered at the notion of such a thought and dismissed it, pleased to instead be sitting here peaceably and taking in the warmth of the morning sun. In spite of all that had happened in the past few days, and still utterly lost in the thick of a wilderness, Turi felt oddly at peace now within this sullen forest. He sniffed the fresh woodland air that was thick with the scent of pines and firs, then peeled the outer layer from another chestnut and bit into it. He had barely a moment to savor its soft taste.

Harsh nearby voices interrupted his brief reverie.

Turi froze, the chestnut dropping from his hand as he caught the sounds of the voices and picked up the choppy lingo he recognized to be that of Dekras warriors. He had heard it enough during the siege of Castle Kathor days earlier. Its contrast to the pattern of those he dwelled among at the castle was unmistakable. He leaped to his feet and scurried off recklessly into the surrounding brush.

Treading a nearby deer trail, three men garbed in the maroon battle colors of Dekras paused as they harkened to the sudden thrashing of brambles and dead branches. Mixed into that panicky flight came also the gasp and whimper of a human voice. With a whoop the three men gave chase!

Turi fumbled aimlessly through the thorny thicket, his face and hands bleeding from twigs and briars snapping out like springs and raking him cruelly. He held back an urge to yelp at the pain and continued in his clumsy flight. Had he showed even an inkling of discipline or caution, he would have avoided nearly running into the creature standing abruptly in the path of his intended escape.

A wildcat ... much like the one from the night before. (Perhaps the very one?) Turi froze in his tracks, then shot a furtive look back in the direction of his pursuers. The wildcat also reacted to the commotion, hissing softly to Turi, then darting off into a thicket. Turi blinked, puzzled by the animal's actions. Was it simply fleeing at the sound of the approaching men or ...

He dismissed the absurd thought from his head. But the tromp and thrash of his pursuers gave him cause to reconsider the absurd. Turi dove into the very brush where the wildcat had disappeared. To his shock (and dismay) he found himself sliding roughly down a weedy gully, crashing finally into a clump of tall brambles. Cursing silently to himself, he glanced about, noting that the wildcat was nowhere to be found. From high above, he heard puzzled angry voices and the spitting forth of unintelligible oaths — giving credence to the stunning success of his clumsy escape route. Turi crouched quietly, unwilling to budge or breathe.

He remained that way long after the men above the gully had apparently left. Quiet returned to the forest. Absently he fingered the haft of the Queen's Dagger. It bristled unpleasantly in response to his touch. A cool surge seeped into his fingers and hands and passed up through his arm. Turi let go of the dagger. Cautiously he eased down onto his belly and slid snake-like through the weeds, away from the direction where he had heard the soldiers' voices.

A fat ground squirrel poked its head out from between two thick ferns, alarming Turi. In spite of himself, he laughed softly at his own skittishness. He watched, amused as the squirrel retreated in reaction to him. Turi rose slowly to one knee, feeling much akin to the woodland rodent he had startled. The surrounding bushes and trees remained sullen and still. Not a sound that even hinted of pursuit. He rose higher into a cautionary crouch and continued on with his stealthy trek.

Turi had crept along in that awkward half-crouch for some time. His back ached as he stole through a grove of low-hanging willows. With no hint of his pursuers anywhere, he finally risked rising from the painful crouch and stepped up his pace. A shout from somewhere nearby informed him he should have stayed low. Panic seized him and he thrashed wildly through the prickly overgrowth! Thorny twigs raked him over the face and hands and cut through where his trousers and blouse were unprotected by the remnants of his leather armor. He clenched his teeth and swallowed a cry of sharp pain that begged for release. The stomp and tramp of feet storming toward him forced him into a grim silence as he fled. Turi's hands flew up in front of his face as he ran awkwardly, stumbling while trying to ward off the constant assault of snapping twigs.

Behind him, triumphant laughter filled the chilly forest air as his pursuers advanced in anticipation of the catch. Turi tripped suddenly on a coiled root and lurched forward over a log, losing his balance. He fell, smacking his face on the hard ground! He yelped then scrambled back to his knees, his face a mask of dirt and blood, some of it seeping into his mouth and causing him to gag. And as he rose, Turi stared straight into a pair of dirty leather britches. His eyes traveled up the rest of the body blocking his path – a stocky, maroon-armored man who hoisted a pikestaff in both hands. The face that glared down at him was crude and hog-like. The ruffian's two companions emerged almost immediately in back of Turi. The hog-faced leader gestured with his pike for Turi to rise the rest of the way.

"Up, Kathorian worm! Much as we despise it, we're not to slay you – yet." Crude laughter followed from all three soldiers. It stung. Flat out humiliated, Turi reacted, surprising both himself and his apparent captors. He reached with one hand for his short sword and, with his other, scooped up a clump of dirt. He hurled the dirt directly into the hog-faced leader's eyes. Turi then lunged forward and swung his sword with the other hand!

The other two soldiers gaped, unable to believe their eyes as the "little Kathorian worm" connected miraculously, catching their temporarily blinded leader with a wild slash on an exposed area of his arm. The leader bellowed in rage and Turi stepped back, also unable to believe what he had just done. No longer laughing now, the other two stepped in and seized Turi. But the leader gestured them off, straining to clear his vision. His puffy face regarded Turi coldly. The other two shrank back as they saw the look in the hog-faced leader's eyes. Turi bit his own lip in fear as the Dekras leader wiped casually at the blood pouring from his shoulder, then put a hand up to his mouth and sipped at it, chortling in mock approval of his young opponent. He smirked and with one hand invited Turi to engage him.

"Come again worm. Let's test your bite on a foe who can see."

"Mind that he lives ..." cautioned one of his comrades.

"Oh, he'll live," the leader seethed.

Turi regarded all three, seeing no option but to play out the ruffian's game. He yelled, again startling all three Dekras warriors, then charged, swinging his sword! But the seasoned leader reacted as the trained fighter he was. He raised his pikestaff and blocked the impending blow. A dull clang sounded as Turi's sword was stopped cold. Turi gaped at the bearish strength of his opponent who did not even flinch. And as though tossing off a sack of clothes, the leader gave a heave of his pikestaff and sent Turi hurtling back, smacking him onto the weedy turf. Turi let loose a groan. His sword went flying. He peered up through a haze at his foe lumbering toward him.

"Best you'd stayed tucked in your hole, worm," the man grunted. Laughter from the other two added to the young man's pain. "And once we –"

A sandaled foot slammed roughly into the small of the hog-faced leader's back, sending him lurching forward and toppling over Turi's sprawled body. The man fell hard to the ground, landing face-first in a nearby clump of prickly briars. He howled morosely as the thorny ends poked into his forehead, cheeks and chin.

Turi glanced up from where he lay and saw none other than... Duwin, the high druid of Kathor, poised close by and garbed in his usual robes, his only armor being a leather doublet and skull cap. In one hand he sported a savage looking scimitar. The other two Dekras warriors gawked — first at the ungraceful sight of their bellowing leader with his buttocks sticking up from the thorn bush, then at the portly druid who appeared anything but a man-of-arms. Duwin gestured tauntingly at himself.

"Send this 'worm of Kathor' back to his hole."

One of the soldiers moved to assist his leader, eying Duwin warily ... while Turi lay on his back, watching, the wind knocked out of him. The soldier helped the hog-nosed leader to his feet.

"We'll see how you fight when someone stands face-to-face with you, priest!" spat the leader, eying Duwin viciously.

"Indeed we shall, pon!"

Outraged by this return insult, the leader burst out with a war cry and charged. He swung his pikestaff in a ferocious swipe at Duwin's head. But with surprising agility the stocky druid ducked and sliced out with his scimitar, catching the man below his leather tunic and above the belt line. Duwin withdrew the blade as the hog-faced leader glanced down in astonishment at his own bloodied abdomen. The man groaned in horror and dismay, then uttered a throaty curse as he collapsed and died on the spot. Duwin turned and waved his scimitar in a mock salute at Turi's other two assailants. The druid spread his arms awide and smiled with mock courtesy, beckoning them to engage him.

Watching in astonishment from where he lay, Turi slid a hand under his vest and touched the haft of the Queen's Dagger — weighing for a moment that he might assist Duwin should the two seek to oblige the high druid in further combat. A queer tingle from the Blade quelled that notion. Turi glanced round instead at the surrounding terrain, considering a conjuring as he eyed rocks and branches and thorns. He tried concentrating but had trouble settling his already frayed nerves. He shook his head in frustration.

"I'll send you back to your hole, worm of a priest!" snarled one of the Dekras soldiers, spurred on by Duwin's taunt. The soldier lunged forward and jabbed fiercely with his pikestaff, but Duwin sidestepped with an unexpected agility for one so stout. He parried the thrust then slid his scimitar down the length of the pike, slashing the man's hand and causing him to drop his weapon.

"A toothy worm though, eh, sir pon?" the druid snickered. Both Dekras soldiers stood there agape, the one clutching at his badly bleeding hand, the other staring back-and-forth between his wounded comrade and the grinning druid.

Both turned and fled.

Duwin appeared almost comical as he moved with the lumbering stealth of a chunky cat, looking this way and that, assuring himself there was no further threat. He turned and, with his usual jovial air, regarded Turi. "It seems I've found you not a moment too soon." There was obvious concern beneath the druid's light tone as he assessed the boy's condition. Turi was unable to respond. He was nearly on the brink of tears as he stood there, so utterly relieved to see his beloved mentor. "You are all right?" Duwin added.

"Yes," Turi barely eked out.

Duwin walked over and helped Turi to his feet, scanning him for injuries. He yanked a water skin out from his robes and handed it to the boy who drank gratefully. "Perhaps it's time we saw more to your skills with a sword, eh?" he added lightly. The high druid twirled his scimitar neatly in the air. "It's good to be adequate at more than one skill."

"Adequate...yes," Turi responded glumly. Duwin smiled reassuringly then reached inside a sack tied to his hip and offered some dried fruit which Turi bit into hungrily.

"Now then, let's to your wounds," said the druid. "It should take but a few moments and then we can —"

"Duwin, sir? Kirspen. She is ...?"

"Alive and well, my boy."

"Where ...?"

Duwin tended carefully to a cut on Turi's face. "She awaits us at the encampment. It's not far, perhaps an afternoon's ride. My horse is nearby."

"Kirspen is there? Now?"

"She is much needed," the high druid said solemnly. "As far as any of us knows, she was the only healer to survive the raids."

Turi shook his head in amazement. "And the King ... ?"

"He awaits us in Gruton," said Duwin. "Men from our village militias have been coming there in response to the riders we've sent out." He paused a moment. "Had we not got word from Lady Jadiane of Thayne's raid, we'd have all been ambushed on our way to Nuwich."

Turi smiled in relief that Jadiane was alive, but he was confused just the same. Duwin read his face and beckoned that he follow. "It seems we underestimated Rojun Thayne," the druid added grimly. "He is a cunning one, that knight. He gambled on our trying that very diversion." Duwin shook his head as though scolding himself. They continued walking through a briary thicket.

"Then if we'd gone on to Gruton in the first place ...?"

"Thayne would have missed us entirely," Duwin responded with a humorless smile. "And our Queen would not have been taken. Ah, but in all his pomp, Sir Rojun did not realize he'd left Lady Jadiane alive. She managed to get hold of her horse and ride to warn us of the enemy's next move. Sir Gaurth went out right away to find the King and turn him toward Gruton with the rest of us."

The path narrowed slightly. "Then the Queen –"

"– is a prisoner in Dekras, yes," Duwin answered, his voice all but breaking. Then he turned and offered Turi a smile. "Eh, you might want to know it was Kirspen who convinced us that some of you might still be alive."

Turi looked at him, pleased. Then a cloud crossed his face.

"It was survivors you were looking for then, yes?" Turi all but whispered, as though expecting Rojun Thayne himself to spring out at them from the brush. "And not the ... not the Dagger?"

Duwin stopped again and stared at him sharply.

"What's that?"

"I ..." Turi paused, drew a long breath, then pulled back his vest, revealing the Silver Blade.

Duwin nearly choked. "Turi, I think you had best explain."

CHAPTER TEN
A Brooding Druid-King

Inside his lore chambers, Kryzol sat up stiffly in his high-backed chair, glowering. His narrow gaze was fixed on Lothi. The wry old druid squirmed uncomfortably under the druid-king's baleful eye. Malbric the Dekras elder and his younger compadre, Suhn, both looked on with an air of solemnity that masked their underlying delight with the newly anointed high druid's discomfort.

"Then you believe this acolyte of Duwin's now has the Silver Blade?" Kryzol demanded.

"I ... yes. That is, one cannot be entirely certain, My Lord. The only other could have been Jadiane."

"The woman-knight, yes. A rare mistake there for Thayne," Kryzol mused. "He is usually more thorough than that." The druid-king studied Lothi carefully, a look hinting of suspicion now in his eyes. "Our horse messengers tell us the soldiers we sent out found nothing more than a frightened pon – whom they failed to capture." Kryzol's tone made it clear those soldiers would pay for their failure. "Possibly this was your young acolyte?" He leaned forward and dropped his voice. "I've lost good men on this venture of yours, High Druid. Men who might have served Dekras better had they been out helping Sir Rojun look for Kieman."

Malbric tittered quietly to Suhn who smirked back discreetly in satisfaction. Lothi simmered from behind his moustache, aware what was going on in back of him and vowing to remember it.

"Lord Kryzol," Malbric broke in politely. "Should we now plan a march to Gruton and destroy Kieman while we have the strength amassed here to do so? Surely this acolyte, this pon that Druid Lothi fears cannot —"

"There is cause for fear so long as Shaikela's Power Root may lie with the enemy!" snapped Kryzol. All three underlings gaped at this rare outburst by the normally poised druid-king. Seeing their reactions, Kryzol composed himself, but his purring voice was yet strained as he spoke. "I myself have never forged a Root so potent. Wielding it would kill most any other druid."

"Then perhaps it will kill this boy," reasoned Suhn.

Lothi frowned skeptically at that assertion.

"And perhaps it will not," Kryzol said solemnly. Lothi smiled. He'd won here and he knew it. So did the other two who exchanged looks of defeat. Kryzol rose, eying all three.

"I will send Rojun Thayne out again." He stared hard at Lothi. "But it is a great risk. With Kieman rousting another army from his surrounding provinces and surviving legions, I prefer that my Knight-Captain were here, mustering our soldiers for the march. Yet the risk is greater with my cousin's Power Root unaccounted for."

Lothi nodded respectfully. He refrained from shooting a smirk back at his rival druids. The other two remained stoic as Kryzol addressed them.

"Druid Suhn, you will accompany Sir Rojun and his men. If this acolyte is as gifted as our High Druid suggests, it will serve us well to have one of cryptic skills there to deal with any mischief he might conjure."

Suhn bowed in response to the druid-king's command. He then paused and drew a long breath before posing a question so softly, it was likely that only Kryzol heard it clearly. "My Lord? Does that mean you will allow me possession of my own Power Root again?"

Kryzol responded with a look that melted the younger man. End of discussion.

CHAPTER ELEVEN
Regrouping

In a dusky glade, Kathorian foot soldiers and knights milled about while others kept watch. Rush torches flared in the failing afternoon light. Turi sat on a rock in a remote corner of the camp, speaking with Duwin while Kirspen held a poultice to one of the deep wounds he had received during his ordeal in the woods.

"Perhaps if I'd not hid for so long like a frightened rabbit, we might be in better position to –"

"If you'd not hid, you'd likely have been killed," Duwin scolded. "Then there would have been no one to keep that Dagger out of Kryzol's hands, as the Queen bade you."

"There's nothing cowardly about hiding if it keeps you from dying," Kirspen added. Turi blinked then stared at her, as though seeing her in a suddenly different light. "And it's no easy feat for someone to stay alive in the woods that long all alone," she added.

Turi blushed, then nodded his head and smiled. "I have someone to thank for that. She's always telling me which plants are safe to eat."

Kirspen smiled back, flattered by his compliment. They were interrupted by the clop and clatter of horse hooves. The rest of the camp was on the alert instantly. Riding down the trail that lead to the glade, two knights approached.

"It's Sir Gaurth!" a soldier cried out.

"And Lady Jadiane!" shouted another.

Turi smiled. A familiar smitten look fell over his face. It did not go unnoticed by Kirspen, still rankled by his usual display of puppy love over Lady Jadiane. She bit her lip in an attempt to quell a flush of jealousy.

Sentries stationed along the trail stepped out to greet the two riders. Gaurth rode a huge coin grey stallion; Jadiane was on her beautiful roan. Both knights wore green-tinted chain mail armor.

They dismounted and walked toward the glade while foot soldiers tended to their horses. His armor clinking in near perfect rhythm with his steps, Gaurth cocked his head side-to-side, causing the bright green plume of Kathor on his helm to wave defiantly. In striking contrast, Jadiane followed in a subdued silence. Duwin, flanked by Turi and Kirspen, walked over to greet them.

"Well, Duwin, I see you've found your bookish apprentice!" Gaurth chortled.

"Indeed. He has survived these past ten days on his own in this forest," the high-druid replied crisply.

"Much to his credit then that he can skulk and hide like squirrels and mice fleeing the weasel," said Gaurth.

Duwin scowled at Gaurth, seeing Turi was hurt by the comment. Kirspen squeezed Turi's arm, gesturing that he disregard it.

"But there's some weasels of Dekras who've learned there's more than mice roaming the Kathorian wood this day," the burly knight added, patting his sword and glancing around imperiously. Some of the nearby foot soldiers and knights echoed Sir Gaurth's bravado and threw up a few quiet cheers for whatever havoc he had wreaked.

Turi noticed Lady Jadiane had remained silent, even sullen. He looked at her questioningly but she was clearly avoiding eye contact with everyone.

"Your grand exploits are always a tale for the telling, my humble friend," Duwin said dryly. "But I've news here for you and Lady Jadiane of greater urgency." He indicated that both knights follow him, along with Turi and Kirspen.

Gaurth frowned and looked to Jadiane, but she simply shrugged and trailed along dutifully with a lackluster uncharacteristic of her.

Turi stared glumly at her. His mind drifted back to a moment both he and Jadiane wanted to forget. He could not wash away the sad image of her being brutally toppled from her horse by Rojun Thayne, nor the sound of the Dekras knight-captain's triumphant laughter.

Turi nodded in understanding as he watched Jadiane drowning in her own shame. His stomach sank. A hand touched him gently. He turned. It was Kirspen. Her chestnut eyes stared into the soft brown of his own, then glanced toward Jadiane and back to him again. She smiled sadly and kept her hand on his shoulder a moment longer.

* * *

In a quiet quarter of the glade, Duwin and Gaurth debated heatedly as Turi, Kirspen, and Jadiane listened. Turi and Kirspen sat on a downed tree, while the rest were seated on large boulders — though Gaurth was constantly up from his seat as he argued with Duwin. Heated as their conversation was, it remained hushed.

"With all due respect, High Druid, the fate of Kathor depends on rousting together enough doughty lads who can swing a sword or nock an arrow," Gaurth insisted, straining to contain his voice.

"The time for such bravado is past, Sir Gaurth. We've no chance if we rely solely on arms to repel the Druid-Lord."

"But —"

"Kryzol has a fully trained army at his command. We do not."

"But our villagers number more ..."

"Against trained warriors led by Rojun Thayne?" Duwin countered. "And if Kryzol does have supernatural aid as we've now heard ... ?"

"We don't know that for sure," said Gaurth. "We have only the words of half-crazed outliers who —"

"Those people from my home village are not as crazed as you say, Gaurth," broke in Lady Jadiane. "My parents are still alive because of them."

Everyone turned and stared abruptly at her.

"Narek is not a hamlet of weak-minded souls," said Jadiane. "Whatever force struck them was real and far more dangerous than any army of 'doughty lads!'"

There was an awkward pause as Jadiane realized her emotions had got the better of her. Flustered she sat back down. Turi stared from one of the two knights to the other, trying to make sense of it all. Duwin took note of his reaction. He turned to his young acolyte.

"There are events that have happened in your absence ..."

Turi scanned the faces of all of them, noticing that even Kirspen appeared evasive when he turned to her questioningly. Duwin addressed all of them, his voice lowered, eyes shifting back-and-forth from the group to the surrounding trees and brush.

"We may have in our possession, now, the one means of thwarting Kryzol," the high-druid said, his eyes resting on Turi. Gaurth grunted quietly to himself, his head shaking with an air of obvious doubt. "You may go ahead and unsheathe the Blade, Turi," Duwin added.

Turi frowned nervously at Duwin, hesitant to draw forth Queen Shaikela's fabled power root. Duwin nodded reassuringly and crossed over to him to mask Turi's actions from the rest of the encampment. Turi hesitated a moment more, then reached inside his tunic and withdrew the Silver Blade. It glowed a bright sheen of silver in the autumn sun. The others gaped.

"So beautiful a blade," Jadiane uttered softly.

"It is indeed," said Duwin.

"A more well-made bodkin I've not seen, I'll fairly admit to that," agreed Gaurth. "But –"

"There are cryptic forces of untapped might forged within this Power Root," said Duwin. "Very few could wield it safely. Its essence is one of pure *quicksilver.*"

Turi stared in awe of that. "Quicksilver is the most active conductor of Living Energy that exists," he said in stunned silence.

Duwin nodded. "And the most dangerous," he added grimly.

"So it is with this ... shining dagger we are to try overthrowing Kryzol and all of Dekras?" Gaurth blurted skeptically, drawing a shush sign from Duwin.

"Make no mistake my friend," the high druid said in a hoarse whisper, "we have strength here more formidable than any castle ever built."

Gaurth frowned again. "We will, of course, see a demonstration of some sort?"

"Gaurth, can you just be silent and listen for now?"Jadiane broke in quietly.

Gaurth did not appreciate the rebuke.

"Mmm ... Easy to see why you would rather put your faith in sorcery now," he quipped.

Jadiane gave him an icy look, hurt by his candor. Gaurth shuffled uncomfortably, knowing his comment came across harder than he had intended. Turi, meanwhile, shot imaginary daggers with his eyes at Gaurth, while Duwin simply shook his head at the knight's inappropriate remark. Embarrassed by his own mistake, Gaurth pressed the issue defensively.

"Just let that bragging lout Thayne show his face when there's a man of equal mettle about ..."

"You may soon have that opportunity, Sir Gaurth!" Duwin snapped. Dead silence fell over the small quarter of the glade. The high druid leaned in closer, hovering over all of them. "I did not say we can prevail by the Silver Blade alone." He drew a breath. "The Queen's Power Root may allow us to stand against Kryzol himself. But it will still take an army to defeat an army." There was another moment of strained silence as his words sunk in. Jadiane spoke first, almost perking now at Duwin's comment.

"If Kryzol himself were defeated, his army might lose heart."

"Indeed they would, Lady Jadiane," said Duwin, nodding.

"But how can this Dagger be used against Kryzol?" Gaurth pressed on as politely as he could. "Our King is no sorcerer and ... and Duwin, you've told me yourself that your own sorcerous skills are few."

"The High Druid has another in mind," Jadiane said wistfully.

Turi started at that. Kirspen, meanwhile, fought off an involuntary shiver as she turned and eyed Turi, fear and concern etched over her face now.

"What riddle is this?" asked Gaurth. He eyed Jadiane annoyingly. "And since when do you know what druids are thinking?"

"The training of true knights requires more than swords and shields," she answered flatly. Her reply drew a little touché smile from Duwin, and Gaurth did not fail to notice.

"Well, I am not shy of a good book now and then," Gaurth blurted.

"That's good to hear, Gaurth," Jadiane quipped. Turi and Kirspen exchanged pert smiles of satisfaction at Jadiane's brief moment of triumph here. Duwin eyed Gaurth the way a schoolteacher would regard a petulant student, then gestured everyone to huddle in closer. Turi still clutched the Queen's Dagger close to his chest.

"Turi, what you've not been told is that several days ago Jadiane's home village of Narek was ruined by a powerful Chinook," said Duwin.

Turi's eyes widened and he stared sympathetically at her. "I ... I'm so sorry," he stammered. "I've heard tales of those dread winds that come down onto the plains from the mountains."

"This is far worse than the tales," said Jadiane. Her tone harbored a chill that sent goosebumps rippling up both his arms.

Duwin slipped in closer to them. "Turi, you've heard me mention in class how one might use the Living Energy of the winds to raise a small storm?" Turi nodded solemnly. Duwin continued. "Queen Shaikela is one who can do just that." He paused, drawing a long breath. "And so is Kryzol."

Turi stared at Duwin, then eyed the tight circle of his companions uneasily, their faces concealing something. Only Gaurth appeared vague, though he wore a solemn look that told Turi something was about to occur of which he alone was completely ignorant. The young acolyte regarded the group with a growing discomfort, a tremor of suspicion creeping over him now. The Silver Blade in his grasp warmed suddenly, then started glowing and pulsating fiercely. Alarmed, Turi tried letting go of it, but it stuck to his chest and hands as though having gained a life of its own. A wave of giddiness lapped over him. Through no will of his own, he pressed the brightly pulsating blade more tightly to his chest.

Duwin's eyes squeezed shut and he concentrated fiercely. Turi swooned abruptly and fell back off the log, but Gaurth was already there to catch him. The burly knight lowered him gently to the ground. Duwin then signaled Kirspen into position. She knelt over Turi, her slender fingers rubbing his brow gently. She turned and nodded to Duwin. Gaurth frowned in disapproval the whole time, while Jadiane simply shook her head sadly. Turi's eyes slammed shut and he lay gently on the grassy turf in an unnatural slumber.

CHAPTER TWELVE
Visions of the Damned

From the moment Turi had swooned and fallen back into Sir Gaurth's waiting arms, he was already in the trance state induced by High Druid Duwin. Visions of a corpse-grey mist swirled before him with the helter skelter fury of a mounting blizzard. Dark figures danced inside the mist as ethereal shapes gradually formed.

* * *

Gaurth's strong hands gripped Turi about the shoulders, keeping him from thrashing around as he lay on his back squirming. The boy tried desperately to turn his head — as though that might dispel the images he was seeing with his inner vision. Kirspen caressed his face while her other hand squeezed his wrist pulse. The Silver Blade rested securely on Turi's chest. Duwin and Jadiane looked on sympathetically.

* * *

The dancing images Turi beheld now took on familiar appearances. Through the misty grey, a party of leather-clad foot soldiers marched triumphantly up a ghostly hill; they followed a swaggering, heavily armored knight whose horse was decked out every bit as martially. Even in his betranced state, Turi gasped as he recognized none other than Rojun Thayne. Something limp lay draped over the horse's shoulders and neck. And then Turi cried out as the limp figure on the horse was revealed to be Queen Shaikela.

The Thayne figure turned and called back to his soldiers, his voice soundless in the misty void. The big knight-captain threw back his head and laughed crudely — audible now as though coming from some distant echo chamber. Turi screamed and the image broke up.

* * *

The betranced Turi squirmed as Kirspen continued tending to him. His friends perceived, partly, the images he suffered as he screamed them out through gasping breaths.

"No! Duwin sir, he has our Queen! Rojun Thayne has Queen Shaikela! Someone stop him!"

Duwin, Kirspen, and the two knights watched and listened painfully as Turi continued blurting out all he was 'seeing.'

* * *

The mist inside Turi's mind cleared, revealing an exquisite looking bed chamber. Strapped by leather thongs to the wide bed, lay a naked Shaikela. A silhouette, cloaked and hooded, appeared. It was bony and tall, raptor-like in its movements as it advanced toward the bed, then discarded its hooded cloak. A faint cry came from Shaikela as the now naked figure leaned over her. It was Kryzol. With quiet menace he eased onto the bed, covering her. Turi moaned as the images broke up ... only to be replaced by others.

A rocky mount now loomed into view, surrounded by a tangled forest. A craggy fortress jutted forth from the mountain, like some alien growth. The image shifted to the summit where, inside a circle of walled rock, lay a vast mound of boulders: cairns, upon which an obsidian altar shaped in the likeness of a winged reptile was built. The glassy altar was smothered in blood runes and rose some twenty-feet from the cairns, hovering over the summit plateau. Its reptilian mouth was frozen in a wide leer. And there stood Kryzol, perched in a groove cut between the two horned ears of the giant stone reptile — his robed arms stretched awide, his head thrown back as he screamed incantations into a stormy night.

To Turi's horror, a limp Shaikela lay at Kryzol's feet.

The violence of the night increased and Kryzol gestured frantically with one hand, while in the other he clutched a glowing object which appeared to be a distortion of Lothi's Power Root. A dirty shaft of wind funneled down from the tumult, striking the misshapen cone and then veering off into the body of the prone queen. Shaikela's body writhed as though caught in the throes of epilepsy. Then abruptly she was sucked up into the turbulent night!

The gruesome image broke up and reshaped into yet another: the village of Narek moments before it had been destroyed by the raging Chinook days earlier. Once again the narrow roads bustled with activity, while a distant speck advanced from across the plain, growing larger as it crept along with a predatory sentience that drew cries from terrified villagers as they sighted its rapid approach.

And lastly, Turi beheld the very top of the funnel: a ghostly face trapped within it — *the face of Queen Shaikela*, twisted and deranged as it peered out miserably from within the twirling mass.

And Turi screamed at the top of his lungs!

* * *

Turi's eyes popped open. He lay on his back in a glut of twigs, Gaurth's strong hands still holding him firmly. Kirspen worked feverishly to calm him, rubbing him about the temples and massaging him over the heart. But he shook violently, still caught in the rift between the tangible world and the *weird* he had fallen into when Duwin had invoked the Silver Blade's cryptic source. Kirspen continued rubbing. She called for mandragora juice which Duwin handed her.

"Is there nothing else we can do for him?" Jadiane asked.

"The girl's doing all that can be done," Duwin replied. "He should ..." The High Druid was not confident enough to finish the sentence. He bore the look of a man who had taken a gamble he might regret. Gaurth glanced up only to scowl, then turned back to Kirspen.

"It's no fault of yours, young lady," the knight said gently to her. "You've done well for yourself here."

Kirspen glanced up at this unexpected, uncharacteristic word of approval from Sir Gaurth of all people. She nodded softly in return.

Turi finally calmed and stared up, seeing Kirspen first.

"I'm very glad Duwin brought you along," he whispered to her, a tiny smile etched on his face. Kirspen smiled back as everyone else breathed sighs of relief. For the moment at least.

CHAPTER THIRTEEN
Dissension

Lothi stood before a band of foot soldiers and knights gathered in the druid-king's courtyard. He was flanked by Kryzol's two other underlings, Malbric and Suhn. No one was warming up to him in the least — and his two rivals watched smugly as the onetime elder from Kathor struggled. A knight spoke up.

"But what of this New Power our Lord Kryzol himself now wields? Surely he can crush Kieman's army of villagers with that alone!"

"Yes, why should we fear this *pon* of Kathor?" quipped another knight, a stoutly fellow. A chorus of grumbles and "Ayes" followed his remark. It flustered Lothi all the more, knowing the obvious pleasure Malbric and Suhn were deriving from this — especially Malbric, whom Lothi knew would have been named High Druid had he himself not come along so fortuitously.

"If we do not capture this ... acolyte," Lothi yelled over them, "there may soon exist another power: one great enough, perhaps, to nullify even that of our King's!"

"That is blasphemy!" snarled the first knight; and others echoed those sentiments. Lothi wondered if he might have to call upon Kryzol himself to calm these men he was expected to lead. And not receiving any help from his resentful underlings only increased the lack of respect shown him by the soldiers.

"It is the truth!" Lothi shouted, mustering some of his gnarly old fire. "It is why the Lord Kryzol has decided to send Rojun Thayne out to lead you again!" The mere mention of the legendary Thayne brought a hush over the group; the name of their fearsome knight-captain not only invoking confidence, but also lending concern that Thayne himself might entertain favorable relations with this newly appointed high druid. Lothi smirked inwardly at the success of his ploy and so pressed the issue. "Or do you wish to see Kieman succeed in his ambition to make Dekras a part of Kathor?"

That provoked a heated response from all of the foot soldiers and knights and even caused Malbric and Suhn to exchange nervous glances — their hatred of the turncoat Lothi overshadowed more by fears of what he had just said. Lothi nodded subtly to himself as he beheld the chattering mob and his now unsettled rival druids. For the moment, he had shown the measure of competency he knew his lord Kryzol had expected of him.

CHAPTER FOURTEEN
More Plots

The camp in the glade was breaking up as the Kathorian foot soldiers and knights prepared for their march back to Gruton. Sounds of swords and shields, clinking armor, horses neighing, and orders being quietly called out filled the air. Near the mid-camp area, Turi rolled up a small tent and bits of camping gear. Kirspen helped him as two stout knights watched over them protectively from a distance.

"You should have seen her face, Kirspen," Turi said softly.

"I'm glad I didn't," Kirspen answered.

Turi stopped rolling up the tent and stared drearily at her, his gaze pained. "She was ... a part of that Chinook, Kirspen," he said, blinking in disbelief at the sound of his own words. "That whole storm was *a living thing.*"

Kirspen looked away, her mind not wanting to accept the horror of what Turi had witnessed for himself.

"That's not the same practice Duwin teaches you, Turi."

"No. But it's what can become of someone born with too much of the —"

"Turi, you could never become like that. You're too decent," she reasoned quickly.

"So was the Queen," he said just as reasonably.

She put a hand to him. "It was the Druid-King's doing." Kirspen gazed around at the breaking camp, wanting to change the subject. "You'll remember what I said about which plants to avoid eating?"

Turi forced a little smile. "Oh, I'll remember."

"And promise that you'll stay close by Sir Gaurth and ..." She paused and drew a long breath. "And Lady Jadiane."

"Believe me, Kirspen: I've no wish to be all alone in the forest again."

Kirspen eyed him darkly, uneasily. "Or in the Marsh Sea."

Turi shivered at her mention of the dreary swamplands. "I'd rather forget that we have to go through there. Duwin's told me many a queer tale," he added.

"And I wish you didn't have to do any of this, Turi. How can they even think of sending you right into the heart of Dekras?" Kirspen was nearly on the verge of tears and her pent up frustration had finally broken through. Turi stopped packing and stared hard at Kirspen. Then, abruptly, he threw his arms around her and hugged her.

"There's no other way to release the Queen," he said simply. She sighed, not liking his answer, but nodded knowingly. Gently they broke their embrace. Turi forced an attempt at joking. "Perhaps if you'd not fed me so many caraway plants last night, Duwin wouldn't think me strong enough for this journey now."

Kirspen smiled. "There is something to be said for healing people." Her chestnut eyes regarded him dreamily; then she leaned over and kissed him. Turi wasn't fully sure what to make of it, but didn't seem to object either. For the first time he appeared to regard his "chum" in a bit of a different light.

In another quarter of the camp, Jadiane walked with Duwin. She was in full battle armor, her helmet in one hand, her long brown locks streaming past her shoulders.

"Then you don't think she's turned to evil?" Jadiane asked as they strode past some sweet-scented pines.

Duwin shook his head and waved a thick finger.

"It's Kryzol's evil craft that made her into what she is now, Jadiane. Remember, Shaikela was greatly weakened when they captured her. And she was without her Power Root when it happened."

Jadiane eyed him wryly. "The cost of forging one of those Roots seems a bit high, mmm?"

Duwin gave a thin smile. "Now you sound like Sir Gaurth."

Jadiane frowned at him. "Gaurth often sees more clearly than he speaks." Duwin waved both hands in lighthearted acquiescence, hearing the tiny edge in her voice. "And what of your own Power Root, Duwin?"

Duwin smiled at her as a father might smile at a daughter. He pulled back his robe, displaying a glowing blue buckler. "You've seen this before, Jadiane. It's beryl, one of the most active conductors of the Living Energy ... but a mere child's toy in comparison to the Queen's Power Root." Jadiane eyed the sea-blue buckler fastened round the high druid's waist, regarding it with an almost childlike wonder. "Ah, if only Sir Gaurth and those others took this sort of interest," he added softly, a clear pride in his tone.

"It's not the way of knights, I'm sad to say," she replied. "Yet, I know Gaurth might appreciate it more if only he would ..."

"There's more in common between druids and knights than either cares to admit," said Duwin, putting an arm around her. "And I'm pleased to say that some knights do see it." He covered the beryl buckler back up, noting a momentary peace returning to Jadian's face. "And you're right, my girl. The cost of forging a Root of Power is high. Once done, *your very essence* merges with it."

"And without it ... ?"

"Why, you are less than you were before forging it," he replied simply. Jadiane's misty eyes brightened abruptly.

"Then Lothi –"

"A weaker Lothi, unfortunately, is still stronger than many who bear their own Power Roots," he said, catching the direction of her thought.

Jadiane sighed and looked away despairingly.

"Of course he's now like an old snake that must dole out its venom sparingly. He is, at least, less potent and more vulnerable."

Jadiane nodded, mildly encouraged. "Kryzol's Power Root, the one we heard Turi speak of ..."

"It's now that Altar he forged," he said grimly. Jadiane wiped her brow nervously at such a thought. Duwin nodded. "It seems he used Lothi's Root, along with those of his other druids, in order to create one so utterly monstrous and potent, thus –"

"Making himself stronger while weakening underlings who might yet think to challenge him," she concluded.

"Ha! Ha! You see, Lady Jadiane, you do understand the ways of druids."

"I'm afraid so," she said, forcing a smile then eying him with concern. "What awaits young Turi now?"

"Too much, I'm afraid. He is a rare one though. No acolytes I've known – and even few druids – have shown the strength to withstand the casting of a weird." Duwin stared at Jadiane, his own sense of guilt clear. "Using the Silver Dagger on him that way was dangerous."

A crackle of leaves and twigs alerted them both.

"Aye ... your mystic eavesdroppings nearly took a fatal toll on the lad." Sir Gaurth, in full battle apparel, emerged from a tiny alcove of bushes where his great grey stallion munched on some tall weeds. Like Jadiane, he carried his helmet in one hand. He stared skeptically at Duwin.

"A risk I did not take lightly, Sir Gaurth," Duwin replied crossly, not liking the knight's tone one bit. "I'd have cast a weird upon myself if such a thing were possible."

Gaurth shook his head, not buying into any of this. "And what of the risk you take now? Sending only Jadiane to accompany me as we deliver your apprentice and that magic dagger into Kryzol's very lair?"

Duwin glanced around somewhat furtively, his expression making it clear Gaurth should have been speaking in more hushed tones. "It will be up to you and Lady Jadiane to see that does not happen. A test of knighthood, yes?"

Gaurth frowned at the druid's implied challenge of his knightly prowess. Jadiane shut her eyes, not welcoming a spat here.

"Remember, Sir Gaurth," Duwin added. "You knights risk only your lives ... That boy risks his soul."

CHAPTER FIFTEEN
Back into the Forest

Fully packed up, the Kathorian force readied for its march to Gruton. Farther up where the glade narrowed back into a woodland path, Duwin stood passing final words with Lady Jadiane who waited by her horse. Gaurth was already mounted, swaggering even in his saddle, his bearing that of a man ready to challenge the gods themselves should they dare question his mettle. Jadiane spoke ever softly with Duwin, clearly not wanting Gaurth to hear — though Turi, standing inconspicuously not far off, was able to catch their words.

"Rojun Thayne ... ?" she queried nervously.

"I cannot say," Duwin replied, understanding the strain in her voice. His brow tightened. "But I think Kryzol would likely send Sir Rojun out to find the Blade," he added solemnly. Jadiane struggled to contain the fear in her eyes which was unmistakable.

Watching and listening discreetly from where he waited, Turi could not help turning away at the supple young woman's sense of dread. Fabled knight of Kathor or not, she was deathly afraid.

"But then it will be all the easier for our own army if Thayne is not there to lead Kryzol's, eh?" Duwin added with mock cheer. His oval face offered an encouraging smile. Jadiane smiled back weakly, then walked over and mounted her horse. "In another day we'll have our forces mustered and readied for battle," the high druid said, turning to address Gaurth as well. "Kryzol will not have the time or the strength to divide his focus. You give us hope."

Duwin nodded reassuringly, getting no reaction at all from Jadiane, and seeing only a despairing look of foreboding from Turi. Even the usual cocksure smirk from Sir Gaurth was absent. The high druid shook his head, controlling his own rising sense of despair, then indicated to Turi that he mount behind one of the knights. Turi drew a long breath, hesitated, then boldly took a step toward Jadiane. He was intercepted by Gaurth's booming voice.

"Come then, lad!" the burly knight called heartily, mustering a bit of his renowned verve. "Climb upon the back of this fine steed of mine and learn how men of might do travel!" He cantered the big grey steed over to the boy.

Turi made no move to mount, thinking he would much rather learn the pleasure of gripping a knightly maiden round the waist as he rode behind her. But that was not to be today's pleasure, so, straining to conceal his disappointment, he struggled awkwardly to climb up into the saddle behind Sir Gaurth. After two miserable, failed attempts that landed him unglamorously on the ground, Turi finally mounted — with Gaurth all but yanking his arm off as he hauled him up behind him. The young acolyte moped as he stared glumly over at Jadiane.

In spite of the gravity of the situation, Jadiane could not repress a shade of a smile, aware of the boy's awkward dilemma.

"Eh ... Turi?" Duwin called up to him. Turi turned clumsily back toward Duwin, almost tumbling from the saddle and drawing a subtle look of reproach from Gaurth. Duwin hustled over with his stocky man's odd grace and helped balance the boy back upright. He handed Turi a small sack. "The rampion roots you liked so much, and more of the caraway plants," Duwin added. "Kirspen was concerned."

Turi nodded, a bit embarrassed. He took the sack while Duwin smiled knowingly. Gaurth watched with a growing impatience.

"Well then, let's be off!" the big knight exclaimed. He and Jadiane both urged their horses into action, waved, and galloped off.

Duwin remained in the same spot for several moments after they had disappeared down the leafy trail. He continued watching well after he could no longer see them, his face now gloomy and grey.

"Farewell my friends," Duwin said quietly, then added under his breath: "I hope I've not sent you on your way to something more foul than death."

CHAPTER SIXTEEN
Squabbles and Dangers

Riding upon his huge black war horse — the steed decked out in nearly as much armament as the massive rider it bore — Rojun Thayne led a contingent of mounted knights and heavily armored soldiers along a worn woodland path. Some of the soldiers were piled into horse-drawn wicker carts, while others hustled along on foot. Young Druid Suhn rode next to Thayne, the two engaging in occasional dialogue, Suhn often dipping his head in agreement. There was no mistaking who wielded the authority as Thayne glanced back, regarding his charges the way a thick-maned lion lorded over its pride. The imposing knight-captain nodded in approval as they pushed on with a predatory deliberation.

Deeper into the woods, Thayne and his procession of raiders gathered themselves together at a crossway of several paths. After a brief exchange, the knight-captain and Druid Suhn led a detachment down one path, while two other groups explored the remaining routes. No alternative was bereft of consideration this day.

* * *

The trio of Jadiane, Gaurth, and Turi rode briskly along a narrow trail. Turi moped silently to himself as he listened, from the back of

Gaurth's steed, to the perpetual squabbling between the two knights.

"There's no need to take offense, Jadiane. I merely point out that if the guard there had been more alert, Thayne might not have caught all of you so unawares."

"And you think the King is to blame as well?" she asked sharply.

Gaurth frowned, then restructured his case. "Eh ... not exactly. He had the well-being of the Queen to be concerned with."

"As did the rest of us, Gaurth."

Gaurth strove to contain his tone. "It's just ... the duty of a knight to be mindful of pending attacks."

"So you do blame me!" she snapped.

Clutching the rear pommel of Gaurth's horse, Turi glanced around at the trees, the bushes, the squirrels ... anything to ·preoccupy himself with something other than the now tiresome debate that had been going on for quite some time.

"No," Gaurth answered flatly. "I do not fault you for something beyond your range of skill."

Turi winced at Sir Gaurth's hard statement, unable to believe he would even say such a thing considering how she already felt. Jadiane confirmed that with an icy look she shot Gaurth. The big knight merely shook his head and sighed.

"Very well then, I shall be blunt."

"Oh, please do," she quipped.

Gaurth forged on, oblivious to her tone. "Your intention to perform your duty in knightly fashion was noble, Jaidane. As was our King's choice to give you that chance. He is a good man. As is evident in how all those provinces dwelling so many leagues away still choose to place themselves under his reign. Kieman has always been justful in his ways — eh, perhaps more than need be."

"Kindly make your point, Gaurth."

Gaurth took a breath and drew himself up higher in his saddle. Turi, meanwhile, squirmed down smaller, wishing not only to hide himself, but to hopefully disappear altogether. He knew what was coming. So did Jadiane.

"The task of knighthood is more suited to men," Gaurth said as conclusively as he could muster.

"Because I failed in mine?" she asked, stung more than usual.

Gaurth started to respond then paused, his hazel eyes looking her over closely. He'd gone too far and knew it. His tone softened.

"Jadiane, you are a very intelligent woman ... as brave as any man." He watched her carefully, noting how she held her face taut in an attempt to maintain resistance to this quieter tact.

"But ... ?" she queried somewhat facetiously.

"But it is more a man's task to protect others from harm," he added with a tone of finality. Turi rolled his eyes in disbelief at the big man's obtuse coup-de-grace. And Jadiane all but smirked at the answer she had known all along was coming. She held up her horse and eyed Gaurth squarely.

"As a man like Rojun Thayne protects others from harm?"

From behind Gaurth's back, Turi smiled at her coy retort. Gaurth fumed, the green plume on his helmet also seeming to snap with annoyance as he turned his head sharply to her.

"That is not the point, Jadiane! What I'm trying to say ..." Their chatter continued on incessantly as they rode on through the woods. It lingered till much later as they passed through a narrow glen. The sour look on Turi's face spoke volumes as they cantered on.

Their banter slipped into a lull as they emerged out from the glen and into a tight enclosure of willows. Their voices fell to more hushed tones within this less familiar terrain. Gaurth, in fact, had fairly ceased, but Jadiane would not let it drop, as though it were her duty here and now to speak on behalf of all women held in check by men. And Turi noted Gaurth's mounting frustration with that.

"If it is the duty of a knight to protect others from harm," Jadiane pressed on, "then all that matters is –"

"– the knight be successful in doing so." Gaurth blurted. Too late he realized he had landed more of a telling blow than intended. The look on Jadiane's face made it clear that if she had not blamed herself for Shaikela's capture earlier, she surely did now. Turi, seeing her reaction to the worst of Gaurth's verbal blunders, shook his head in angst, regretting that he himself was not capable of clouting Gaurth over the head.

Gaurth, meanwhile, sighed loudly and looked away, not at all pleased with himself. He glanced somewhat sheepishly at Jadiane – and the two of them exchanged a look different in nature than any other Turi had noticed previously. The young acolyte looked from one to the other, puzzled. He wanted to say something, ask either —

His thoughts were interrupted suddenly by the clop of horse hooves behind them. Gaurth's head snapped round like a wild beast sensing a predator. Turi tensed, frightened. And Jadiane all but froze in her saddle. A name barely whispered forth from Turi's lips.

"Rojun Thayne ... ?"

Neither of his companions responded. Jadiane turned uneasily to Gaurth. "Dare we wait and see?" she asked almost inaudibly. Gaurth looked back at her. There was no mistaking the fear in her eyes. Turi saw it too.

Gaurth turned his coin grey steed toward the sound of the approaching hooves, his martial blood rising. He eyed the narrow path behind them, his ears attuned to the faint clatter of horse hooves and the creak of wooden wheels kicking up dirt and stone. And Sir Gaurth of Kathor knew it could only be their enemy in pursuit of them. His was the face of a man who hated to flee, yet one who also knew the futility of making a stand that would accomplish nothing. He turned his head to regard the scared boy behind him, glanced again at Lady Jadiane battling her own resentful fears, then patted his steed on the neck as though confiding to a comrade.

"Another time ... another time," he whispered soothingly to the great war beast. Gaurth spat bitterly. The sound of approaching horses and riders grew louder. "Come, it's not far to the Rocklands," he said with reluctance. "We'll lose them in its maze." He veered his horse round and led them quickly down the narrow trail.

Clinging tightly to the knight as the great stallion galloped on, Turi's head was awash with many confused thoughts.

* * *

A vast maze of boulders and cliffs, bordered by the forest, composed what many folk referred to simply as the Rocklands. In some ways it appeared manmade, its formations carved seemingly into an architecture of intricate narrow paths that wound through like uncoiled snakes prowling the towering grey mounds. And high above, nooked inside a narrow fissure where two enormous boulders overlooked the stony trail some thirty-feet below, Gaurth, Jadiane and Turi, still mounted, waited as they peered down in deathly silence.

They had not been there long before they sighted a party of mounted knights leading a company of soldiers riding in horse-drawn wicker carts, while others ran alongside them on foot. Even from their stony perch above, the three could make out the bright maroon garb of Dekras. The martial company passed along the trail without so much as an upward glance. Gaurth bit down on his lip as he muttered softly to the other two. "It does not appear Thayne is among them." He shot a sidelong glance at Jadiane, as though probing for a reaction, but her green eyes remained fixed nervously on the party of warriors passing below. Turi, meanwhile, looked sick with fear at the sight of so many of Kryzol's denizens out searching especially for him. And where was that dread beast of a knight-captain if not here? The boy shivered involuntarily.

Gaurth could not help observing the mantle of fear creeping over both his comrades. His face grew somber and grim as he glanced around at the narrow fissure in which they hid. "This is as good a place as any to camp tonight," he said finally. "I doubt they'll search for us up here." The other two both seemed relieved by that, though Sir Gaurth did not share in their relief.

CHAPTER SEVENTEEN
The Rockland Night

Night was upon the Rocklands. The campfire around which Sir Gaurth, Lady Jadiane, and Turi huddled was but a faint speck under a sky illuminated by stars and the full moon. The three ate morsels of fire-toasted meat and nibbled on dried fruits, while occasionally partaking in modest portions of mead. They were camped in the lee of a rocky overhang which helped mask the presence of their tiny fire.

Jadiane was quiet and sullen, while Turi listened wide-eyed to Gaurth who was enjoying more than his fair share of the wineskin's contents. "And then in full armor, mind you, the knight-in-training is required to scale a wall and then run into the fray of a mock battle," Gaurth boasted softly, mindful of his voice level.

"Without pause?" Turi asked wide-eyed.

"Without so much as lifting his visor," Gaurth answered.

"And then is he a knight?" said Turi.

"Ooh — no, lad," said Gaurth, sitting back and taking another sip of mead from the wineskin. "That's just the beginning of proving he's fit to travel the road that awaits him."

Turi thought he caught a brief look of annoyance from Jadiane at Gaurth's exclusive, ongoing references to knights as males.

"There's more than martial ways to the manly practice of knighthood," Gaurth said grandly, the mead warming him all the more. "There's chivalry too! From the time he's a mere varlet, the youth who longs to be a knight must seek out a lady of fair stature to be Mistress of his Heart. And it's to her he commends the purity of his deeds."

Jadiane rose abruptly and busied herself with a sudden interest in gathering firewood. Turi noticed, but by now was overwhelmingly caught up in Gaurth's rousing account of knighthood.

"And you have such a lady, Sir Gaurth?"

"I do," said Gaurth, reflecting on that for a moment. "Though another would have been my first choice, had she not decided to ..." The big man's voice trailed off suddenly and he cleared his throat somewhat uncomfortably. "Well, eh, it's not important I suppose."

Turi eyed him, puzzled. "Who then is —"

A loud thump and several conspicuous snaps cut Turi off as Jadiane had returned and dumped a load of wood down near the fire, part of which she trampled on while also breaking a couple long limbs rather loudly. Gaurth merely nodded to himself knowingly. He moved to change the subject.

"Eh ... lad, tell me something of the druid's training then, for I'll fairly admit I've probably not kept as close a look on that as I should."

"Or other matters," Jadiane muttered quietly, eying Gaurth in a way that caused the big man to squirm in a fashion uncharacteristic of him.

Utterly caught up in the dialogue, Turi failed to notice the subtleties going on between the two knights. He drew a long breath, feeling awkward at Gaurth's inquiry of his druid training after all the bombastic talk of knighthood.

"Well, sir, there's not any of the wrestling or riding that knights do," Turi stammered. "But there is more swordplay than you might have thought."

Gaurth's ears pricked at that. Turi blushed.

"I've just not been very ..." His voice faltered some as he regarded the legendary Sir Gaurth eying him with a new curiosity, which, although it flattered him, made him uneasy just the same. He shrugged awkwardly, not wanting to embarrass himself here. "What I mean to say is ... there may be ways in which druids and knights are more alike than either realizes."

Gaurth smiled with an air of genuine intrigue. "I would hear this," he said. Turi's eyes widened with pleasure, having expected the knight to snicker at such an inference. The big man's warm hazel eyes, instead, encouraged the boy to explain further.

"Well, sir, you mentioned that the, uh, varlet ... ?"

Gaurth smiled and nodded in acknowledgment of his using the correct term.

Turi continued. "Well, if I understand correctly, the varlet who hopes to be a knight is required to know something about the mysteries of the forests and the rivers and hills. Yes?"

Gaurth nodded again, listening even more intently. This even drew a knowing smile from Jadiane as she eavesdropped and appeared to sense where Turi was going with his comparison.

"Well sir, a druid must become almost a part of nature itself," said Turi. There was a moment of sustained silence in which Gaurth stared at Turi with an air of budding respect.

"Do druids choose to be this way? Or are you born to such things?" Gaurth asked soberly. Turi paused again, containing his excitement at Sir Gaurth's sincere interest. A glance toward Lady Jadiane thrilled him all the more as it seemed she too was every bit as interested.

"Well," said Turi, "you've both heard Duwin speak of the Cryptic Sense ..."

"All too often, I'm afraid," Gaurth injected lightheartedly. "But how did you first know you had this 'sense?'"

Turi drew another breath, hesitant to explain so personal an aspect of himself. He eyed Lady Jadiane again and she smiled at him reassuringly. "It's something you just ... feel," he said so softly the words seemed to fall from his lips and be carried over by way of the gentle breeze. The two knights listened with even greater intrigue. Turi pushed on. "You see, when I was young — just a boy, back in Nuwich then — I sometimes felt strange things happening inside me, especially when I walked in the woods. The voices of the animals and the birds ... they were like songs in my head. I could nearly understand them. And sometimes it seemed as if the trees all around me ... even the rocks ... the ground itself was so ... active. I know now, from Duwin, that those were my first experiences with the Living Energy. Druids believe it exists in all things."

Turi looked to see if they followed him, and was encouraged that both knights appeared fairly spellbound now. He marveled inwardly and hoped they were not just humoring him. Then again, Sir Gaurth especially did not seem to be that type; and Lady Jadiane was far too polite to deceive anyone.

"I remember when I first tried explaining all of this to my parents and their friends," Turi went on. "It made them nervous. They said people would think I was a witch, or that our family bore the blood of the Dekras Cult. My parents grew frightened by it all. With Nuwich being so far from Castle Kathor, not much was known about the ways of the druids at court. I suppose that's why people in distant hamlets like Nuwich are called bumpkins," he added, for the first time a hint of bitterness in his voice. The change in Turi's tone caused the two knights to eye each other and Gaurth contained a tinge of guilt he felt, having used the word bumpkin all too often in the past when speaking of village outlanders.

"We never knew much about anything except what happened right in our own little villages," said Turi. "If Duwin hadn't gone out looking for young people who bear the Sense, I'd have just kept on believing something was wrong with me."

A bird squawked suddenly from up in one of the sparse nearby mountain trees, startling all three from their reverie. Gaurth's hand had gone instantly to his sword and he flushed with embarrassment at such an action. "You've a strong sense for telling a poignant tale, lad, if it can draw me in deeply enough so the chirp of a mere bird puts me at arms," Gaurth chuckled, easing his sword back into its scabbard. Jadiane gave a quiet giggle of her own at hearing Gaurth even admit to such a thing. "But do go on," the burly knight added.

Turi smiled thinly in appreciation of Gaurth's words, and then his tone darkened again. "I suppose I'd have stayed as ignorant as the rest of the folk from my village, had Duwin never come there." His eyes nearly watered as he continued. "Duwin taught me it's not freakish to be different."

Jadiane studied him closely, noting how the boy's gaze switched back-and-forth between her and Gaurth. Then finally Turi stared straight into the smoldering campfire. "He said I should think of it as a *gift*."

Gaurth shifted uneasily on the rock where he sat, his face taking on a more somber look during Turi's last statements. He and Jadiane exchanged another brief glance; then the big knight turned and, he too stared into the depths of the fire, pensive and inward. Jadiane rose and stalked over to Turi, kneeling beside him and touching him on the arm. Turi's heart fairly danced through its next few beats as she spoke softly to him.

"Never feel you're freakish because you're not like others, Turi," she murmured. Turi lost himself in the soft leafy green of her gaze. And little else that happened afterwards, before he finally rose and found his way to his bedroll, mattered to him at all.

It was the dream that later came to him, unbidden and plaguing his sleep, he wished he could have forgotten.

CHAPTER EIGHTEEN
The Unbidden

Turi strolled down a winding path of tall firs and handsome spruce, the trees murmuring quietly like friendly sentinels greeting him as he passed blissfully beneath their boughs and leaves. He took in the sweet autumn scent that wafted out from those leaves ... from the bark of the trees ... from the very soil itself, a scent he had taken in on many a walk through such woodlands over the past thirty years. It brought back fond memories. Memories of an aging old druid who had taught him the love and lore of Nature and how to ingest its gentle might; and to wield it as though painting with a soft, potent brush. How often that elder druid had spoken to him of this wondrous gift – in particular during a time when a wielding of the Cryptic Sense oft meant something dangerously different.

From somewhere a bird chirped. And within the nearby brambles and brush, some small mammal – perhaps a rabbit or a fox – scampered by. He peered curiously, merrily into a patch of thick ferns – and what peered back at him did so with eyes that were not friendly. Druid Turi blinked, then took a sharp step backward.

The eyes in the patch of blackening brush smoldered with a pale fire. They were hostile and filled with a queer hunger. Turi felt a chill creep up his spine. It rose from the ground and whipped up through

74

his legs, into his back, and paused just near his neck. He glanced down and gasped as he saw that a snarl of rampant bittersweet vines had coiled round his ankles and slithered up his legs and back; then, with a hiss, the vines looped round his neck and slid back down toward his hips, binding him, seeking ... something.

Turi tried to scream, but his lungs were soundless. He heard, instead, a cry of horror from within the confines of his own head. The woodland world around him bore no sounds of its own now. Save one. A cold voice spoke from somewhere, speaking words meant only for him. Words making him understand that the gentle walk he had started here would never come to pass. A fearful glance upward assured him so. The surrounding spruces and firs that had sung so gently to him earlier — welcoming him like an old comrade — now groped at him with twisted limbs, the way vultures might grope at a dying creature.

And the ugly voice spoke again.

* * *

Turi woke with a jolt. Sweat drenched him and he glanced round in a near panic, his eyes straining to see anything with a familiar look. Finally they caught the shape of Sir Gaurth's broad back, illuminated dimly in the faint moonlight as the big man sat stolidly on the rim of where Turi, Lady Jadiane, and the horses slept. Gaurth stirred and glanced back, ever vigilant, seeing nothing other than Turi sitting up. The knight raised his head to the boy curiously. Turi drew a breath of relief in the knowledge it had been but a cruel nightmare and simply waved to Sir Gaurth that all was well.

Gaurth turned back to face the dark and whatever lurked out there in its shadows. And Turi lay back down, not to sleep another wink that night.

CHAPTER NINETEEN
The Marsh Sea

The trio rode through a rocky gully, eying warily the overhang of boulders and cliffs. It was chilly and grey and the morning mist bit into them. Turi especially shivered in the wake of the disturbing dream he had the night before. The vivid recollection of what seemed so frighteningly real still lingered in his mind. He had chosen not to share it with his two knightly comrades. Instead he occupied his thoughts with the impending trek that would likely prove far more disturbing, given its material essence.

"So you've both crossed the Marsh Sea before?" Turi asked Gaurth, more and more awed by the big man's past exploits.

Gaurth nodded nonchalantly. "It was an actual crossing back then," he smiled. "Ferryman made a good wage of it too. Merchants all used the Marsh for passage to the outer provinces, and druids even rafted through when they wanted to fetch their queer plants and the like. But it's grown too dangerous of late."

"So King Kieman had secret paths cut through the woods that could be used instead," Jadiane chimed in, as though mildly miffed at Turi's growing fascination with Sir Gaurth.

"Why aren't we seeking one of those paths then?" Turi asked, frowning.

"Because they take too long," said Gaurth. "And Kryzol will expect that. Ah, but he won't expect us to dare ferry the Marsh Sea itself now."

"I suppose not," Turi said nervously from behind Gaurth on the saddle. The mere mention of Kryzol's name brought back a silent rush of the dream images he was still trying to suppress. And the very next statement from his own lips made him all the more uneasy. "Duwin says druids avoid the Marshlands now because it's become a ... glut of Living Energy gone foul."

Both knights winced at Turi's sordid description and Gaurth pursed his lips unpleasantly as he tossed a wry look back toward him. "Well, it was never a pleasant place to begin with," the knight quipped.

It was late afternoon by the time they reached the banks of the gloomy Marshlands. The horses whinnied uneasily as they emerged from a canopy of willows and onto the banks of the Marsh Sea. Flying insects zoomed everywhere, humming and buzzing while scuffling noises in the undergrowth suggested the presence of other unseen life forms.

The entire region reeked of swamp stench — plants and wood that had rotted and were covered in aged mold. Turi shuddered as something with a large sound to it slapped through the nearby murk. Impervious to any of this, Gaurth turned his head, indicating it was time to dismount. Turi nodded uncomfortably and climbed down, his eyes darting about. He took a tentative step toward the shore

"Come ... time is short," said Gaurth, dismissing any hope the boy had of turning back. The big knight gestured for Turi to untie the saddle bags strapped to the horses, then walked off toward a section of the bank cluttered with heavy brush. Turi watched as Gaurth searched the bushy area, then apparently saw what he was seeking. Effortlessly, Gaurth heaved away some of the rubble, uncovering a large, rickety looking raft moored to a long tree root that poked out from the foot of the slope. The makeshift craft looked as though it had not been used in years.

Turi groaned silently to himself as it was clear they would soon be embarking on this flat jumble of knotted logs that did not appear capable of even holding them, let alone bearing them across the gruesome marsh. Miserably he began untying the saddle bags, but halted abruptly as though seized by an invisible pair of hands! His body twitched involuntarily. Within the folds of his clothes and belt, he felt the Silver Blade pulsing. Then just as abruptly the bizarre seizure was over. Jadiane was at his side instantly and Gaurth hustled over to join them.

"Turi, are you all right?" said Jadiane, gripping him gently.

"What is it, lad?" Gaurth asked, the strong hazel eyes peering into Turi's, one hand on the boy's arm. Turi merely stood there, held up by the two (and leaning deliberately on Jadiane); he blinked his eyes.

"I ... I'm not sure," Turi answered. He regarded them both sheepishly as they guided him to a rock where he sat. "It felt almost as it did in that queer dream last night, but ..."

"What dream?" snapped Gaurth. "You said nothing of this before, least of all last night when I heard you wake."

Turi eyed them uneasily, realizing now the folly of having kept his nightmare from them. "I ... it was just a dream, or so I thought. Brought on, I supposed, by all our talk of druids' ways ..."

"And yet you felt no need to –"

"Gaurth please," Jadiane urged quietly, putting a hand softly to his arm. Remarkably, the big man simply threw up his own hands and turned away. Jadiane reached over and ran a finger over Turi's cheek. She stared deeply into his eyes. "Please tell us, Turi."

Turi felt fully ashamed now as Sir Gaurth turned back to face them. Both knights leaned over him eagerly. "There's so little of it I can recall," Turi explained slowly. "It seemed I was older and walking in the woods. But then the woods changed little-by-little all around me. It felt like it wanted to attack me. Part of it even grabbed at me, and, and, it reached for ..."

Turi stopped as he felt his hand sliding over to where the Silver Blade was strapped to his hip. He shuddered as the motion made him recall the gnarl of vines slithering down toward it in the dream. He strained to remember more of the fading nightmare. "And I heard a voice. It spoke softly to me, but it was cold and cruel. It told me I would 'join the Queen where she was' and ..."

Turi buried his face in his hands and Jadiane held him tightly. Gaurth's scowl faded and his face softened. "It's all right, lad," he said. "Likely just a nightmare brought on by ... "

"No, I don't think so, Sir Gaurth," Turi said firmly, his head popping up to face them again. The two knights regarded him more curiously. "It was more than a nightmare. I'm sure of it. But this just now ... this wasn't the same." Turi tensed. He twitched as though feeling out the very air around them. "There is quicksilver here," he said strangely.

Gaurth and Jadiane eyed one another uneasily, then turned back to Turi. The boy was perspiring and on the verge of fainting. Gaurth leaned over confidentially to Jadiane. "If this lad has the mystical innards everyone says he's got, then there's more than a mere find of that druid's metal here ..." He made as if to go on, then paused, regarding Turi once more. Gaurth's sandy eyes took in the trees surrounding the swamp. "We best make haste," he grunted.

"Gaurth, what is it?" said Jadiane.

"Later," he answered. "Let's tend to the boy and be off."

CHAPTER TWENTY
Into the Marsh

The raft measured some twenty-feet in length and fifteen across. It squeezed out reluctantly from the muddy bank, creaking its way through the reeds and marsh grass as though in protest. Standing in the rear, Gaurth hefted a long quarterstaff sort of pole in both hands. He eyed the surrounding woods suspiciously as he paddled.

Both horses sat on all fours in the center of the raft, their forelegs tucked under their massive bodies. Their glossy eyes peered nervously out into the swamp. Jadiane patted them both, offering soft words of comfort, then walked off toward the fore of the raft and stared outward, lost in her own thoughts.

Several feet from where Gaurth paddled the flat craft, Turi sat with his back propped up by a pile of haversacks and other gear. He watched Jadiane cross by, then glanced over at Gaurth.

"Fear not, lad," said Gaurth, catching his look. "I traveled on this very craft with a full scouting party but a few years ago, and it didn't sink then."

Turi smiled skeptically at Gaurth, looking anything but reassured. He bit down on his lip, then rose and walked over to the horses. Tenderly, he rubbed each round the neck then took a deep breath and stalked carefully up behind Jadiane who still stared out at the water, seeing nothing. Sounds filled her head though: the clatter of battle, the cries of warriors and the shrieks of victims, the thunder of horse hooves and, above all, a harsh laugh of triumph and mockery that rose over the rest of the din. Her head dropped and she put a trembling hand to her forehead.

"The horses are very nervous," a voice said from behind her, breaking into her troubled thoughts. The battle din in her head faded. Jadiane turned. Turi stood there awkwardly, groping for something else to say, but unable to come up with it. She closed her eyes, opened them, then nodded solemnly. Turi waited for her to speak but she dropped her eyes down, unwilling to hold his gaze. His heart sank and his next words came out instinctively before he could stop them. "You're nervous too?" He thought he saw a slight bristle. Turi wished at that moment he could have flung himself back over to where Gaurth was paddling, or, better yet, off the raft altogether.

Jadiane's head rose back up slowly and Turi braced himself for the admonishment he felt coming. Instead, she merely looked at him with eyes that clearly said 'yes' and turned away. The steady lap and splash of Gaurth guiding the raft through the rank waters dominated the next few uncomfortable seconds. Then Turi reached over and, very carefully, touched her on the arm. It felt lithe and smooth and he could not repress a quiet rush within himself. If she noticed his silent reverie it did not show. Instead, Turi heard Lady Jadiane sigh as one does when the truth is so overwhelmingly cruel. She spoke without looking at him.

"There is a fear I've not known before. Not until Rojun Thayne ..." She glanced back to see if Gaurth had overheard; but the big knight continued paddling, his gaze fixed ahead on the banks of both shores where the twisted limbs of firs and oaks hovered over the water in the shape of a gangly tunnel. Jadiane paused and followed his stony gaze, noting the ominous look of the approaching concave of trees. Seeing nothing of menace, she turned back and now stared straight into Turi's eyes. "Oh, I've faced foes before who were stronger or faster, even more skilled with the blade than I, but ..."

Again she was at an abrupt loss of words and it was all Turi could do to restrain himself from leaning over and trying to comfort her with a kiss. (Or so he did in his mind at least.)

"Lady Jadiane," he said in as wistful a tone as he could muster.

"You cannot hope to defeat everyone. I don't think even Sir Gaurth truly feels that —"

"You're kind, Turi. But you don't understand." She looked out into the dusky water again, her voice straining. "I was beaten soundly by that brute. I was nothing but a toy in his grasp."

Her words stung sharply and he lost all sense of inhibition.

"But that could happen to anyone," he said passionately. "It happened to me. When I was in the woods and those soldiers —"

"Turi, a pon cannot possibly understand ..." She stopped, realizing what she had just said. She may as well have slapped him with a hand wet with swamp water.

"I ... forgive me, Turi. Please. I didn't mean it that way."

He nodded in a pat response, though the damage had been done and it was clear. The boy's dignity dissolved into dust.

"Would you sit and hear me out?" she said, reaching over and taking his hand in hers. She bid him sit beside her on the raft logs. Unable to believe this gesture on Lady Jadiane's part, Turi knelt, then sat down before his jellied legs collapsed on him. She smiled and he surrendered to it, smiling back. She eyed him tenderly, for the moment more caught up in how she had hurt his feelings than in the mire of her own glum thoughts.

"It's just that your strength is of a different sort than ours ... than of a knight's. You could no more have fought those soldiers than Gaurth or I could match skills with a druid."

Turi weighed the words she had chosen, not offended by them. He nodded in understanding and flashed a fraction of a smile. He turned and glanced out at the murky waters as the raft rippled through, no other sound penetrating the growing dusk except the hum and buzz of flying insects. He sensed she had more to say.

"I always craved the sacred duty of protecting others," Jadiane began softly, again glancing quickly over to where Gaurth paddled silently, quite obviously not wanting him to hear. "My friends all had laughed and said things like 'a beautiful young woman should plan her life more sensibly.'" She drew her head up proudly. "But my father never laughed when I told him kings and druids and knights were what I dreamed of."

Turi blinked in astonishment, then stared with eyes that were all the more smitten as she continued.

"But now I have disgraced that service," she added sadly.

"And do you think I'm proud that I cowered in the weeds when Rojun Thayne attacked?" Turi protested in her defense. "I hid there while warriors like you and Druid Mur fought bravely. I cowered in those bushes while my friend Kirspen cried for help!"

Turi's voice had gone up loud enough so Gaurth, over at the rear, now pretended to hear nothing as he guided the raft steadily toward the rapidly advancing tunnel of trees. He never looked over at the two. A glance in Gaurth's direction by Jadiane, though, signaled Turi to keep his voice lower. He pursed his lips in embarrassment.

"Turi," Jadiane all but whispered, "you showed courage when you took up the Queen's Dagger and kept it from Kryzol's soldiers."

"And you showed courage when you rose up after the battle and climbed back onto your horse to go warn the others," said Turi, surprising both himself and her.

Across the raft, Sir Gaurth gave a subtle smile of approval as he steered the raft toward the approaching alley of wooded banks, never giving hint of having heard a single word.

Jadiane, taken off guard by Turi's comment, tried shrugging it off, but he would not let it rest at that.

"I don't think it's a test of arms that makes Lady Jadiane a knight," said Turi, "but her love for her people."

Her eyes fairly widened at that and she regarded him warmly, more, for the first time, as she would an adult. (And from the rear of the raft, a look oddly of the same ilk came from Gaurth.) Jadiane also saw there was more than affection in Turi's gaze and, despite being moved by it, shifted smoothly to another subject. "The young healer ... Kirspen is her name?"

"Yes," Turi answered, surprised she brought this up.

"She is your friend?"

"Yes. She is a ... friend," Turi answered, still puzzled.

Jadiane put a hand to his shoulder. "There's a touch of something very nice I've seen between the two of you," she whispered.

Turi sighed in full acknowledgment and resignation, his face making it clear he had hoped this discussion was leading somewhere else.

"I ... well, yes," he stammered. "But I think that's because we've known each other well these past couple of years and —"

"She's very attractive Turi. I think you're both fortunate to have found each other." She smiled at him once more, a smile Turi recognized as the sort a teacher gives a lovestruck student. He nodded once more in acknowledgment as the raft bore down on the tunnel of drooping trees ahead.

CHAPTER TWENTY-ONE
Company

King Kieman and High Druid Duwin stood upon the battlements of the walled city of Gruton, Kathor's strongest province and where it was expected the forces of Dekras would strike next. Kieman was garbed in the chain mail armor he had worn previously and Duwin was decked out in his usual woolen robes and leather battle tunic. Standing beside them were two province overlords of Gruton; they were dressed as one would expect of dignitaries – silken caps and samite coats and leathern leggings, men more accustomed to making decisions on matters of city functions as opposed to military engagements.

Though the walled province was well garrisoned and equipped with catapults and other war engines, events of a martial nature had not happened there in some time. Even with Kryzol and his mysterious cult dwelling across the Tundra all those years, it was a distant enough trek and a time long enough past since any semblance of war had been waged. Military preparations had therefore been more precautionary, more ceremonious. Till now.

Perched on the battlements, while horns alerted the combined army of villagers and soldiers into mobilizing for action, Kieman, Duwin, and the Gruton dignitaries stared out grimly at a scene that was now anything but ceremonious – something they would not have imagined even a year ago.

"And how long, Sire, before you think our foe will make his move on us?" Duwin asked, biting his lip and staring out over the wooded horizon, as though expecting at any moment the denizens of the druid-king to come bursting out from the trees.

The king of Kathor turned solemnly, his demeanor displaying the regality expected from one of his stature, in spite of the drab, timeworn look that had characterized him for years. Those who knew him were fully aware how deceptive and misleading that look really was. Kieman's lips pursed and then pressed into a wry smile. "That will be determined by how predictable we are in our next move."

* * *

The raft bearing Turi, the two knights, and their horses, coasted on beneath the canopy of trees. It was dark now and only the glow of the full moon streaming between the overhang of crooked branches kept the watery path fairly lit.

Standing at the center of the raft with the horses, Turi was rubbing Sir Gaurth's stallion round the neck when a sickly whine from Jadiane's roan distracted him. He turned to see the roan was up on all fours now, its eyes shining like prisms of glass. A deathly quiet had crept into the air, a chilled calm that felt rank and unclean. Turi saw Gaurth's stallion rise too. Both horses bristled nervously.

Turi glanced back at Jadiane standing near the fore of the raft and staring outward, still lost in her own thoughts. His urge was to go over and yet try consoling her, but he knew it would prove neither a remedy nor a gesture fully appreciated beyond what he had already said. Instead, Turi turned back and patted both horses reassuringly.

He sensed a queer change in their breathing. His gaze shifted over toward Gaurth. He was startled to see the big man had stopped paddling. Gaurth was eying the rear corner of the raft. The horses also stared in that direction. Turi's eyes followed theirs and his throat knotted up.

A shape crouched in the rear corner of the raft: something woolly and squat.

Turi blinked uncertainly, trying to discern between what his eyes informed him and what his brain disputed. He glanced back toward

Jadiane and saw she had yet to notice. Turi grimaced as his gaze shifted again to the rear corner and beheld that something did indeed lurk there ... something harboring an air of menace. With great deliberation and caution, Turi inched his way over toward Sir Gaurth.

The pale eyes of the intruder, a primate of sorts, followed Turi's every move. Turi eyed the creature back nervously. He blinked as he saw it was wearing what appeared to be the remnants of leather armor.

The raft coasted out from under a tangle of thick branches and was bathed instantly in the light of the full moon. The creature shifted and squinted uncomfortably under the sudden stab of milky light. And Turi saw it was indeed armor the crouching biped wore ... a faded maroon in color. The young acolyte gaped in shock. The face that stared back at him from under a torn skull cap was hairy and filthy; long nails poked out from its fingers and from the toes of its bare feet. In one "hand" it grasped a broken pickax. Turi edged closer to Gaurth, then risked another glance to the fore of the raft and saw Jadiane, alerted now, and also eying the squatting creature.

"It is a pon," Turi heard Gaurth utter softly.

"What?" he replied hoarsely, his eyes back on the crouching figure.

"One of Kryzol's," said Gaurth. "Look at the armor." The creature glared at them more savagely, aware they were talking about it. "Kryzol is cunning," Gaurth continued softly, his eyes never leaving the odd creature. "He sacrifices his pons to block passage through the Marsh."

"What ... happened to it?" Turi asked just as softly.

"Come, lad. You're the druid's apprentice, not me."

The creature bristled more menacingly, as though having picked up on Gaurth's words.

"This is the work of that corrupt energy Duwin spoke of," Gaurth uttered quietly. Turi shivered and turned his eyes slightly toward Gaurth, seeing the big man's face and knowing he did not jest. "And you see that pickax?" Gaurth added. The creature tightened its grip on the pickax, its mouth turning down into a cold sneer. "Kryzol had reasons other than ambush for sending them here," Gaurth added, his hand poised on the pommel of his sword. And with a bloodcurdling cry the deranged-looking biped sprang!

At that same instant, two more dropped down from within the thick branches of a shoreline oak. Others, all looking like the first, leaped out from the thickets and brush along the right bank! The creature that had first slipped onto the raft landed almost on top of Turi, knocking him away from Gaurth and back toward the rear of the raft. Two other attackers sprang directly between Turi and Jadiane. One wielded a broken sword, while the other brandished only its fractured teeth and its long nails.

Another of the mutated Dekras pons landed on the bare back of one of the horses, the roan. Two others rushed in to flank the first creature which, having sent Turi sprawling, rose back onto its feet and assumed a hunched fighting stance in front of Gaurth. But the brash knight of Kathor was not one to be made timid by mere pons – mutated or not. He whirled the long steering pole in his huge hands as though it were a true quarterstaff, flattening his woolly assailant with a smashing blow that sent it toppling off the raft and into the murk of the swamp. Without pause, Gaurth dropped the steering pole and unsheathed his broadsword.

One of his two remaining assailants wielded a rusty spear while the other was weaponless. Gaurth turned to regard the one with the spear. And at that moment, the other one sprang, latching onto the knights armored shoulders and waist. It clawed and bit at him.

And at the center of the raft, Jadiane's roan bucked and reared, trying to eject from its back the woolly biped that clung there like a bug – while Gaurth's grey stallion swung its great head round, trying to get into the fray and butt the creature off its companion's back.

Jadiane, fighting from the fore end of the raft, whirled her longsword in a pattern that fairly mesmerized one of the snarling pons menacing her. Before the onetime foot soldier could even muster an attack against her, Jadiane brought the sword down and plunged it deep into its stomach. Her would-be assailant gurgled pitifully and sank down onto the lashed logs of the raft.

And rising to his feet after the blow he had suffered from the first pon, Turi found himself trapped between Jadiane's battle and the fray with the horses. He stood with his right hand frozen to the pommel of his short sword. The crazed pon facing him was armed with the pointy broken haft of an ax. The creature glared at Turi, causing the boy to tremble with a mix of pity and fear, making him hesitant to draw his sword. Turi's hand slid instead to the handle of the Silver Dagger. It warmed strangely as though in warning. He released it and took a step back. The pon sprang! Turi was knocked flat onto his back as the woolly biped hovered over him, rasping triumphantly. But a loud bawling distracted Turi's assailant. The pon turned its head and Turi instinctively followed its gaze.

Jadiane was standing triumphantly near the edge of the raft, sword raised overhead as she kicked the pon she had just disemboweled into the water. The pon hovering over Turi snarled at the sight of its comrade's demise and launched itself, instead, toward Jadiane whose back was turned away. The pon's sharp ax haft was raised high, poised for a blow to the back of Jadiane's neck.

"No!" cried Turi. He shut his eyes tightly and muttered something foreign, words he himself barely recognized. A surge ripped through his body and ... a narrow spit of water sizzled up from one side of the raft like a hissing water snake. As though acting of its own volition, it shot straight into the eyes of the pon that was attacking Jadiane from behind. The mutated pon yelped in pain and dropped its weapon, its eyes burning from the sting of the tainted marsh waters. Jadiane turned sharply at the sound of the cries. She gaped at the sight of this wooly, armed remnant of a man clutching its own eyes and screeching like a beast of the wild!

The deranged pon that had wrapped itself round Gaurth was pressed tightly to the big man like a giant spider. Its comrade hoisted a spear, waiting close by for the first opening it might seize. Gaurth's cape had been torn free and even part of his mail armor was damaged by the constant clawing and biting. The biped that was stuck to him tried bracing itself for better leverage and placed one of its bare feet back down onto the raft momentarily. Gaurth responded by stomping on it with the heel of his boot! The pon wailed, falling off Gaurth's back, then made another mistake by leaning over to grip hold of its crushed foot. Gaurth stomped down again, only this time on his foe's exposed neck, breaking it. The dead pon's comrade, still waiting close by with spear in hand, gawked and backed fearfully toward the edge of the raft.

Near the center of the raft, the roan struggled with the pon that still clung to its back like a stubborn rodeo rider. The horse bucked again, but was unable to lose the burdensome creature tearing and clawing through its mane and biting down into the nape of its neck. The roan snorted violently and reared up onto its hind legs — then fell deliberately onto its back, crushing the clinging rider beneath its massive equine weight! The roan rolled free and scrambled back onto its feet. Gaurth's stallion sallied in and finished up by punishing the limp pon with a flurry of pounding hooves.

By now, the one pon left facing Sir Gaurth had backed to the very edge of the raft. Another step would land it in the swampy mire. The woolly biped did not appear to want any part of the reeking murk, but seemed to want even less of the swaggering warrior advancing on it. Gaurth did not fail to notice.

"Come, you cowardly ball of dung," he taunted, then spat contemptuously onto the raft logs. "Let's finish this now."

The mutated pon stared uncertainly at Gaurth. It tried growling a warning at the advancing knight, a sound that was bestial but pathetically still human. Gaurth simply sneered and charged. His sword crashed down, slicing through the pon's battered leather helm and cleaving the creature's skull! The half-cloven body jiggled and danced obscenely before finally collapsing onto the raft.

And as Gaurth hollered in triumph from the rear quarter of the raft, the pon that Turi had blinded with a watery spit of Living Energy flailed and clutched haplessly at its own eyes. Turi watched wide-eyed as Jadiane, with the cool deliberation of a seasoned warrior, waited patiently for the right moment then stepped in and casually lopped off the gyrating creature's head. The headless body took a few drunken-like steps then pitched forward, landing barely a few feet from Turi. Turi took one look at the headless corpse, then turned and retched onto the floor of the raft.

CHAPTER TWENTY-TWO
Quicksilver

The raft coasted on through the woody tunnel, bathed in the leprous light of the full moon. Gaurth and Jadiane were clearing the raft of pon corpses and debris while Turi sat clutching his stomach. The horses stood back-to-back like a pair of vigilant watchdogs. Jadiane slipped over to Gaurth as he hefted up another pon corpse, as though lifting a sack of garbage, and hurled it overboard.

"He saved my life," she said softly. "That thing would have had me from behind had Turi not acted when he did."

Gaurth nodded solemnly, then gave a light smirk. "Yes, he spared me having to go over and settle things for you." This time, Jadiane appreciated Gaurth's lighthearted bravado. She punched him playfully on the arm, then they both turned to regard Turi.

The young acolyte still sat near the center of the raft, holding his stomach.

"He's no soldier ... but he's no pon either," Gaurth said, a hint of pride in his tone. Even in his state of misery, Turi caught enough of their words to feel a degree of strained comfort. He could not suppress a sliver of a smile at Gaurth's morsel of praise and tried mustering a semblance of composure as they walked toward him. He eyed them both apologetically, hoping they would not scold him for his unglamorous condition.

"I didn't mean to ..." Turi's voice trailed off as he tried to avoid glancing round where he had emptied the contents of his stomach. Jadiane knelt down beside him.

"Thank you for saving my life, Turi," she said, kissing him on the cheek and leaving him quite unable to respond. Gaurth actually smiled then turned and rubbed both horses gingerly round the neck, talking so soothingly to them, Turi could not believe the cooing sounds were coming from Sir Gaurth himself. Gaurth caught the look on Turi's face and stopped abruptly.

"Well it's best we finish clearing this filth away," the big knight said matter-of-factly. And with that, he hoisted up the headless pon and hurled it callously over one side of the raft. Turi watched in amazement at the man's casual manner. "You understand now," asked Gaurth, "Kryzol's reasons for sending his lower minions into this hell swamp?" He tossed another of the onetime Dekras foot soldiers into the gruesome murk.

Jadiane helped Turi to his feet as they both looked at Gaurth curiously, neither sure of what he was getting at.

Gaurth all but snickered, his usual wry tone returning. "Why, your druid's metal. Your precious quicksilver," he added flatly.

Turi frowned, still befuddled, but Jadiane nodded slowly as it gradually dawned on her. "*Mining*," she uttered, astonished.

"That's why some of them had pickaxes for weapons," said Gaurth. Turi and Jadiane both regarded Gaurth with astonishment. He gave a small, crooked grin in response. "Well, even those of us who bear no trace of this 'Cryptic Sense' can guess right at some things. I think Kryzol has been sending his pons in here for some time. And not just to catch anyone trying to cross –"

"But anyone else trying to mine the quicksilver," Jadiane broke in. "Those tales of druids and acolytes who never returned ..."

"It's likely the real reason he wanted this war. So he could mine this foul place freely and have all that druid's ore for himself," said Gaurth. "Paying no heed to what it did to his minions."

Turi's head spun at the implications of all that Sir Gaurth had just said. "That would give him absolute power," Turi murmured, sweat breaking through every pore of his body. "Power gained from sacrificing his own men. Could their lives mean so little to him?"

Gaurth chuckled humorlessly to himself, then heaved another corpse overboard while Jadiane turned and tended to the horses. She, too, was unsettled by what Gaurth had deduced. Turi edged his way toward her, but was distracted by a queer flapping noise coming from the rear of the raft. He halted and listened more intently, his eyes shifting there nervously but seeing nothing. He drew a breath, then stalked over and peered past the edge, seeing the headless corpse Gaurth had tossed overboard earlier. It was stuck to a large splinter poking up from beneath the raft's water level. Turi's stomach turned sourly, his nose taking in the moldy reek of the marsh and the stench of human remains torn asunder. He felt bile rise up in his throat and forced it back down again, not wanting to give another display of retching in the presence of these two bold knights.

Instead, Turi forced himself to lean just over the rear end of the raft. Again he saw the headless corpse fluttering in the raft's soft wake like a skimming stone. Nausea slipped over him once more, but he fought it off and dipped his hand into the gurgling murk to free the corpse from the splinter. And as he did, something slimy and rough rubbed against his hand. He jerked it back instantly! Turi clutched at his hand, examining it to be certain nothing was wrong with it, then stared apprehensively back into the murk.

He saw a snarl of coiled shapes slithering round the trailing corpse of the headless creature as it flapped along behind the raft. There was the chatter and chomp of many teeth being gnashed as flesh and bone was stripped viciously from the corpse. In a matter of moments, all that remained was a single bony hand still clinging to the splinter.

"'Tis an evil place for sure," he heard Gaurth mutter from behind him. Turi turned and gazed up at Gaurth who merely shrugged, then savagely kicked the head of the last Dekras pon overboard.

The young acolyte watched, unable to turn away from the gloomy spectacle as the woolly head of the pon slowly sank, its sightless eyes still opened wide and staring blankly back at Turi ... as though promising him the gruesome odyssey was far from over.

CHAPTER TWENTY-THREE
A Reluctant Betrayal

The mountain fortress of Dekras loomed tall and cold against the backdrop of the dusky forest that surrounded it. It loomed there exactly as it had in the vision Turi had suffered while caught in the grip of the weird that Duwin had cast on him days earlier. It was the same craggy Keep the young acolyte had seen jutting forth from the mountainside, like a sickly alien growth.

The Druid-King Kryzol stood upon the battlements of that Keep, staring out over its high turreted walls and into a bleak night. The older druid, Malbric, waited beside him, solemn and ill-at-ease. "There's been no word yet?" said Kryzol.

"None, Lord," answered Malbric. "But it's only been –"

"I need to know something soon, Malbric."

"Thayne will not fail you."

"No. I do not suppose he will," said Kryzol. "But that still does not tell me what Kieman has raised for an army — nor what deviltry that acolyte of Duwin's stirs against us," he added with an air of impatience. "I was able to probe his cryptic essence with a random weird that menaced him as he slept, but it did not help me locate him."

The frustrated tone of his reply disquieted Malbric. "A messenger will arrive soon," the elder druid said, knowing his attempt at assurance sounded forced.

Kryzol turned to him, a queer light in his eye. "I can no longer afford to wait for messengers. The knowledge is needed now."

"But Sire, it simply isn't possible," Malbric said softly, apologetically. Kryzol eyed him hard, not liking the man's answer. The older druid withered. "My Lord, to acquire such knowledge without benefit of a spy's report — or having at least captured one of the enemy — you would have to cast a weird on someone. And even then..."

Kryzol nodded in solemn agreement. A knight appeared silently from the shadows. Malbric caught the sudden movement. He glanced instinctively across the turreted walk and saw two more knights of Dekras step out from the shadows, swords drawn. A frosty sweat broke and spilled over the elder druid's face. He whirled back to see Kryzol staring at him raptor-like.

"Lord Kryzol, surely you don't mean to ..."

The druid-king eyed him impassively, his lips pursed as though fighting off a grimace.

Malbric pleaded. "Sire, I am not a young man. I've not the strength to survive ... a weirding," he reasoned desperately.

No response.

Malbric panicked. "Oh please, do not do this!"

When Kryzol replied, his voice was measured, but with a rationale sounding more like a man yet trying to convince himself.

"Our younger druids are too lacking in depth," he said evenly. "Suhn might have served, but he is with Thayne. Therefore —"

"Lothi then ...!" Malbric surprised not only himself with his desperate interruption of the druid-king, but also the knights moving steadily in on them. Kryzol noticed their astonishment at that.

"My own High Druid?" the druid-king replied with more of the icy calm expected of him. "I think not."

And Malbric saw that no sense of protocol mattered any longer here. "He is from Kathor!" the elder druid roared. "A traitor!"

"But I have need of him," Kryzol answered, his tone yet affected and lacking its usual air of genuine detachment.

"And me?" Malbric cried. Have I not served you well these many years?"

"Indeed you have, old friend," said Kryzol, wishing dearly now that he had broken this to the older druid privately. "But the fate of our kingdom is at stake here." He turned away a moment, noticing the three knights still waiting, watching closely. He fixed his gaze back on Malbric, then spoke quietly and firmly. "A sacrifice is needed ... for the good of Dekras."

Kryzol nodded to the knights and they closed in on Malbric who crumpled, weeping, onto the stone tiles of the battlement floor. Kryzol himself seemed nearly on the verge of weeping along with him. But he knew better and simply waved the three knights off with their burden. When they had gone, he turned back toward the southern horizon and gazed coldly that way, promising silently there would be those who would pay dearly.

CHAPTER TWENTY-FOUR
An Enemy Waiting

An icy rain beat down on Jadiane, Gaurth, and Turi as they disembarked from the raft, the horses snorting with relief as they were led back onto solid ground. The chill rainfall gave the marsh an even more sullen look and not a word was spoken as the three mounted the steeds and made off along another narrow woodland path. They rode, barely speaking, until dawn began to break and they saw, finally, a faint parting of the trees ahead. Gaurth indicated quietly that it bordered the open plain leading to the rear of Castle Dekras. And despite knowing that the most perilous, most foolhardy part of their journey still lay ahead, it was tempered by their knowing, too, that they would soon be away from this oppressive Marshland Forest. It gave them a momentary sense of respite they had not felt since leaving the protective shelter of the Rocklands. And it took their minds momentarily from the forthcoming, unknown danger of reuniting Queen Shaikela with her Power Root.

Gaurth pointed down the trail toward a hilly plain just beyond the last of the trees. Drawing closer to the rim of the woods, they glimpsed in the near distance the rear of the dark mount upon which Castle Dekras itself was built. The craggy fortress across the plain was abutted by a mournful looking woodland that was a perfect fit to the corpse-grey mountain from which it sprouted.

A sudden blare of horns jolted them from their thoughts.

"Dekras warriors!" Turi said nervously. Gaurth and Jadiane listened intently. They were little more than a quarter-mile trek across an open plain that would lead to the very slopes of Castle Dekras. Raucous voices rang out in the chill morning air. They came faintly at first, fainter than the trumpeting horns. And then the three heard the distinct clamor of weapons striking armor and shield.

"Warriors," said Gaurth, "but not just those of Dekras."

More horns blared. "Those are the horns of Kathor!" cried Jadiane.

Gaurth grinned broadly. "By the gods, Kieman and that fossil of a high druid have done it!" he boomed. "Our army is here and now engages Kryzol's!"

Turi looked from one to the other excitedly.

"We've outmaneuvered those bastards at last," Gaurth shouted triumphantly. "Now let's to that haunted mount of Kryzol's and finish this business! Hah!" And with that, Sir Gaurth urged his horse out from the woods and onto the plain, Turi holding on for dear life.

"Gaurth wait!" Jadiane yelled as she followed. "We still –" But her voice was lost in the thunder of the horse hooves as Gaurth urged his steed on all the more.

"Not long now lad and you'll be working that druid sense –"

The burly knight's words were cut off by another cry from Jadiane. Gaurth and Turi both turned their heads to see – charging out from behind a pair of hills and cutting them off – a band of some fifteen Dekras soldiers. A number of them were on foot while others rode in horse-drawn wicker carts. They were flanked by a mounted druid. And emerging last came Rojun Thayne himself, riding brazenly upon his armored steed.

"Shall we always be trapped like rats?" Gaurth cursed, glowering from beneath his helm at the advancing ambush. Turi practically sobbed as he watched Thayne and the hooded druid position their men strategically, blocking off any hope of escape.

And even from that distance, Turi and the mounted druid eyed one other. Turi felt, more than saw, the gleam in the druid's eye. His hand slid involuntarily down to the handle of the Silver Blade. The mystical weapon thrummed vibrantly as before. Turi bit his lip nervously, but did not let go this time.

And Lady Jadiane, seeing Rojun Thayne, froze ... while Gaurth reigned in his horse, waiting for the Dekras raiders' next move.

"Easy there, lad," he said quietly to Turi, feeling him tremble from behind him in the saddle. "They've not got us yet."

Turi marveled at the big knight's unrelenting courage and nearly smiled in spite of their plight. He turned and glanced over at Lady Jadiane. His heart all but stopped. For there she sat upon her horse, clearly rigid with fear. Turi shut his eyes, hating to believe it. He had but a moment to react, for in that same instant, Druid Suhn raised a long bony finger and pointed it directly at him. A tingle raced through the young acolyte as he dismissed Jadiane's reaction.

Seeing Suhn's gesture, Rojun Thayne nodded and, with a wave of one hand, indicated to his men they move apart and let him see to this deed alone. The soldiers halted and drew back in compliance. Thayne reared his horse up and urged it out in front of them, twirling his deadly morning star in a mocking challenge at the trapped trio ... then charged.

Caught off guard by Thayne's abrupt move, Gaurth looked to Jadiane ... and saw little more than a rabbit trapped in an open field, dreading the hawk swooping down on it. The usually bombastic knight of Kathor all but winced at her now helpless state. He frowned hard as he heard Turi gasp from behind him. "Hold tightly, lad. I'll not let that swine get at you," Gaurth vowed solemnly and raised his broadsword in defiance of the advancing knight-captain of Dekras.

Trapped and with no time to dismount safely, Turi gripped the back of the saddle, his fingers all but digging into the leather. He shook his head in awe of Sir Gaurth, but could not bring himself to turn and look at Jadiane again.

Rojun Thayne bore down on them.

Gaurth held up his sword, ready to meet the first swipe of Thayne's lethal morning star; but just as he closed, the Dekras knight-captain shifted his attack and went for Turi instead. Gaurth groaned. With only one chance of keeping the hissing chain from wrapping round Turi and yanking him from the horse, Gaurth let go of the reins and twisted his own body back in an effort to shield Turi. The long chain wrapped savagely round Gaurth's waist, the spiked ball on the end slapping down hard and making his mail breastplate ring. And before Gaurth could react, Thayne jerked viciously on the morning star, yanking the big Kathorian knight right out of his saddle. Gaurth crashed roughly to the ground.

He heard the dull crack before actually feeling it. So did Turi; and so did Thayne. Gaurth groaned as the snapping of bone tore through his lower back region. He reached down in a futile attempt to ease the pain he knew was there to stay. It stabbed through him with every move he made, yet somehow the big knight struggled lamely to his feet. And he heard, rather than saw, Rojun Thayne trumpeting at so seemingly easy a conquest.

Gaurth glanced round anxiously for Turi and saw the boy had somehow managed to stay righted in the saddle while the grey stallion galloped safely out of range. And through a muffled fog in his head, he heard Jadiane calling to his horse. Gaurth turned his head toward the sound of her voice ... and saw she had retained enough composure to summon the stallion and Turi away from their would-be captors.

Satisfied with that much at least, Gaurth nodded in grim approval then turned back to face his triumphant foe.

"Dismount and meet me on even terms — Rojun Thayne!" Gaurth punctuated his own taunt by forcing himself into a painful, erect stance. He waved his broadsword menacingly. His stallion meanwhile had brought Turi back, with Jadiane directly behind them.

"There are no even terms, fool!" Thayne roared in response, then raised his great arms awide, looking every bit a servant of the hellworlds. And he charged, whirling the deadly spiked ball. Half-lame, Sir Gaurth stood his ground and awaited him.

Turi turned back to Jadiane in a desperate plea. "Lady Jadiane, please ..."

The plea died in his throat as he saw she was no longer there. Turi stared for what seemed a much longer time at the empty spot where Jadiane had been only a moment earlier. And then he gripped the pommel of the saddle savagely. "Cowards ... Cowards all of you, but for Sir Gaurth!" He reached down and yanked free the Silver Blade, clutching it firmly in his grasp as though daring it to resist his intent to wield it. He held it aloft.

And as he did, he thought he heard Druid Suhn and the Dekras soldiers now hollering frantically. He drew greater strength from that and dismounted, nearly falling in the process. Turi felt himself trembling, resenting that feeling as he waved the Silver Dagger defiantly at Rojun Thayne himself. "Some of us will die with a fight, you plated bastard!" he yelled in a voice he could not believe was his own. But Thayne merely ignored Turi and bore straight down on Gaurth, the lethal morning star twirling viciously once more.

Gaurth held himself as firmly as his battered frame would permit, sword poised in both hands. And all the while, Suhn and the Dekras soldiers hollered desperately, indiscernibly — their words lost in the din of the conflict. *They apparently saw the galloping red roan that Thayne failed to notice.* The Dekras knight-captain was too focused on Sir Gaurth standing lamely but defiantly before him in his green chain mail armor, the Kathorian knight making a human shield of himself that blocked Thayne's path to Turi.

Rojun Thayne swung the deadly morning star down at his lame foe who was equally focused on him, but ... a longsword intercepted it! The morning star chain wrapped round the sword like a frenzied snake, aborting the attack on Sir Gaurth.

It was Lady Jadiane — with a blindside strike at Sir Rojun!

She dug her knees into the sides of her horse for added leverage; then, with both hands, yanked her sword hard in the direction of the morning star's lethal circle. And in nearly the same motion, she let go, causing the combined force of Thayne's last swing to jerk the morning star free and send it sailing off with her longsword!

As though a switch had been thrown, the warning cries of Thayne's cohorts ended. Thayne sat there weaponless and dumbfounded.

Lady Jadiane spat contemptuously off to one side. "Even terms now — swine of Dekras!"

And while Thayne was distracted by Jadiane, Gaurth struck! He lunged painfully over to the Dekras knight-captain and swung his broadsword at his back. A thunderous clang rang out as Gaurth connected with the full force of his body weight behind the blow!

It was followed by the impossible sight of Rojun Thayne tumbling out of his saddle. The dreaded knight-captain landed with a resounding thud, winding up flat on his back! Weighted down by the cumbersome armor, he looked comically like a giant turtle that had been upended.

Gaurth did not hesitate. Ignoring the searing pain in his hip, he lumbered over to where Thayne had fallen and loomed over him, sword raised high as he scanned for breaches in the thick, black plate armor.

"Gaurth — under the shoulder!" Jadiane called out to him. Overly eager herself now, Jadiane dismounted and drew out her dagger. But Gaurth was already on the move. He spied a telltale fissure between the armpit and sleeve of Thayne's breastplate ... a lethal thrust if he was accurate and fast enough. He raised his heavy broadsword, gripping it firmly in his steady hands and, with all of his magnificent strength, plunged it deep into the narrow gap. Thayne howled! The mournful cry was both alien and obscene coming from the mouth of the black-plated giant. Without pause, Gaurth followed up by jerking his own dagger loose and driving it through the eye slits of Thayne's visor, burying it to the hilt as blood squirted out in small streams.

Rojun Thayne's massive body gave one spasmodic heave — and died.

For one frozen instant, no one on the plain moved — not even the horses — as though halted in a bizarre tableau and posing for some gruesome painting to be completed. It lasted but a moment. Then, as if a collective nerve were pinched, a mix of reactions burst loose within Thayne's group. Several panicked and fled, while others weighed whether to follow or rally in revenge of their fallen leader.

Druid Suhn simply stared in disbelief at the impossible. Dread thoughts of how he might explain this to Lord Kryzol himself raced instantly through his brain. Who might possibly have planned on or even imagined this?

Abruptly, one stout-heart among the Dekras group banged his sword rhythmically against his shield in an attempt to rally the remains of the raiding party. Some caught on and readied themselves. But Suhn hesitated, still uncertain what to do. Rojun Thayne was dead. Killed by a trio of badly beaten upstarts.

Across the field, Gaurth and Jadiane hovered over Thayne like a pair of jungle predators following a kill. They turned sharply at the sound of the banging, as did Turi. "It's not over yet," muttered Gaurth.

"There are no more than ten," said Jadiane. She gestured callously at Thayne's corpse. "And this brute alone was worth that many himself."

Turi, meanwhile, stared sullenly across the plain, his eyes fixed on Druid Suhn who watched the three of them from his horse. "And one druid," the young acolyte said softly, more to himself. His two knightly comrades looked to one another, nodded affirmatively, then stepped out toward the Dekras soldiers. Jadiane raised a long, slender arm and beckoned their foes to dare attack as Gaurth bent down to retract his sword from Thayne's body.

And staring out at the mounted druid, Turi felt himself filled suddenly with the same reckless urge. He brandished the Silver Blade over his head, then stepped out in front of Jadiane and Gaurth.

The dagger glowed with a bright silvery hue as though on fire.

"Turi ...!" Jadiane cried as she caught his move. But the boy either did not hear or simply paid no heed as he eyeballed their mustering foes almost contemptuously.

"Come — you pons of Dekras!" he cried out, then turned his gaze upon Druid Suhn. "And you too, lackey of Kryzol's! Come feel a taste of the Queen's Silver Blade!" And as if taunting the mounted druid, Turi waved the glittering dagger round his head.

Across the short stretch of tundra, Suhn listened in stunned silence to Turi's taunts, his eyes fixed all the while on the very object of his quest. How was it that a mere stripling — only moments earlier a terrified child — could now wield so potent a Power Root? Truly there were forces at work this day beyond anything the Druid-King himself had anticipated. Suhn watched, amazed, then gasped.

"Come you —" Turi continued to shout, then halted abruptly.

Incredibly, more of the Dekras soldiers were backing away. The mounted druid turned and followed them, until nothing more than a small group remained to (possibly) continue the fight. Turi blinked, then smiled wryly to himself, reining in the Silver Dagger and holding it up in front of his face as though he and the fabled Power Root were old allies who had vanquished many a foe together. He turned back smugly to regard Jadiane and Gaurth — and nearly toppled over at what he saw.

For there he beheld what had really shaken the Dekras soldiers ... and the hooded druid too. There stood Sir Gaurth, one hand gripping the thick hair of a massive head smothered in blood, which he held aloft: Rojun Thayne's head, lopped free of its body, the bearded face staring sightlessly out into the plain.

"Here is your hero!" Gaurth boomed. "Dare you fight with those who bested him?"

And Jadiane chimed in too. "Come, wretched pons! We'll add your miserable skulls to his and let our druids feast on your souls!"

Turi shuddered at the words she shrieked into the cold tundra air, sounding more like some banshee spirit of the late autumn wind than the elegant lady knight of Kathor. But it had the desired effect on their already shaken foes. The scant remains of Thayne's rattled men scrambled into their wicker carts and fled, leaving only a few resolute souls to face the two knights and Turi. Annoyed that these remnants of the Dekras raiding party would still even consider an attack, Turi advanced toward them.

"Turi, come back. You're not needed for this!" Jadiane yelled.

Turi halted and spoke without looking back. "But I want to help. I'm ready to –"

"You're needed at the castle summit," Jadiane insisted. "Kryzol's druid rides to warn him!"

Turi turned back to her. She gestured across the plain. He looked to where she pointed and saw Suhn riding off toward the castle. Meanwhile, the four remaining Dekras warriors moved cautiously toward the three Kathorians. Turi caught their movements, and marveled at their courage in spite of it all. "They're no cowards, these four," he uttered softly, a tone of reluctant admiration in his voice.

"And we will deal with them," Jadiane said solemnly.

"She's right, lad," added Gaurth, lowering the lopped-off head of Rojun Thayne. "Your courage is needed elsewhere now."

"But what will happen to you two?" Turi insisted, shivering at the gruesome sight of Thayne's head dangling at Gaurth's side. He turned away and eyed, instead, the advancing footmen of Dekras, young men perhaps not so unlike himself. "Sir Gaurth is injured and –"

"Don't worry, Turi. I'll see that this clumsy lout doesn't injure himself further," quipped Jadiane, forcing a jestful smile. "Ha! And he makes a big enough shield to cover me should I need one."

"We'll see later who covers who," Gaurth retorted lightly.

"Be sure not to limp then, 'my hero,'" Jadiane chirped.

And at that moment, Turi realized, for the first time, the true relationship between these two knights. It smacked into him like a wave splattering onto a shoreline, causing him to momentarily forget the crisis they still faced.

Gaurth brought him back quickly to the task at hand. "All right then, lad. No sooner than we engage them, you turn and run for that castle. Duwin said a narrow path in the rear winds to the summit. We'll follow if we can."

Turi swallowed hard, gazed once more toward the foot soldiers closing on them, then looked back to Sir Gaurth and Lady Jadiane. He nodded solemnly. "I ... yes, I'll do it." He sheathed the Silver Dagger.

"Then off you go," said Gaurth. Jadiane smiled at Turi who caught one final glimpse of the Dekras soldiers as they rallied and charged — just as he turned and fled.

CHAPTER TWENTY-FIVE
Lamenting the Dead

Kryzol stood near a wide sterile bed where the limp body of Malbric lay in a tangle of heavy straps, now unfastened. The two knights Kryzol had admitted into the chamber flanked him, awaiting his orders. He spoke softly, more to himself and to the body of the dead druid than to the two men waiting behind him.

"He is dead now ... but a good deal more was learned than expected."

Both knights nodded mechanically.

"Well, old friend, you proved more durable than I would have thought," Kryzol continued. "A pity we did not have this need some ten years past. You might have withstood such a night's work." The Druid-King paused and wiped at his eye. "I'm sorry ... you deserved better." He turned his head slightly, as though quietly including the two knights in the private conference he held with the dead man. "But Kieman and Duwin shield no more secrets now. Their underlings have wreaked a great mischief upon us, oh yes," he added with a rising malice.

Kryzol took another moment to recompose himself, then turned to face the two knights directly. He gestured gently toward the body of Druid Malbric. "You may remove him now." The druid-king turned and walked over to a tiny arched window and peered out at the breaking dawn as the knights hefted Malbric up. "He will be burned later with all due ceremony and honor," Kryzol added with quiet deference. "Druid Malbric may well have saved us all."

Both knights nodded with a matching respect and hoisted the dead druid's body gently away.

"And send the High Druid in to me," said Kryzol. "The greater threat lies elsewhere now."

CHAPTER TWENTY-SIX
Perils Mounting

Dawn broke over the bleak tundra leading to Castle Dekras, revealing Kathor's recently mobilized army — a mix of soldiers and civilians — engaging Kryzol's legions. The druid-king's denizens were already significantly reduced from their initial conquest of Kathor. That in itself gave hope to the attacking force as King Kieman and High Druid Duwin both directed battalions of their mixed army's surprise assault.

Morale was high amongst the Kathorians. But the Dekras forces, minus the fierce leadership of Rojun Thayne, and no longer bolstered by the imposing presence of Kryzol and his two right-hand druids, lacked the sense of conviction shown in their previous battle. Still, Kieman and Duwin both knew better than to draw abrupt conclusions. The Druid-King was not one to unleash his full might early in the battle, as they already so painfully had learned. They pressed their attack nonetheless, with thoughts of past circumstances ever in mind.

* * *

Turi strained as he raced toward the rear slopes of Castle Dekras, gasping heavily as he gazed up at the homely peaks of Kryzol's mountain-fortress. He shivered at the sight, then glanced back out at the plain. Through the haze of dawn, he could make out nothing more than the lumpy shapes of hillocks which blocked his view of the ambush site he had fled earlier. He heard the clamor of battle from the other side of the mount and wondered whether Duwin and the King were now leading the remnants of the Kathorian army to a miraculous triumph, or if Kryzol once again thwarted them with his usual cunning and military savvy. But at least the forces of Dekras no longer boasted the prowess of the monstrous Rojun Thayne, Turi thought with some satisfaction. That comforted him as he pressed on.

Turi turned his gaze once more toward the lower slopes of Castle Dekras, where a jagged path wound up the woody mountainside. He nodded his head and made off in the direction of that path.

* * *

Riding among the ranks of archers who were mustered together on the outskirts of the battle – the main fighting having moved closer to the foot of the castle – Kieman and Duwin surveyed the results of their shifting strategies. Their mix of military and civilian militia had, thus far, held its own against Kryzol's more hardened legions, though both men knew that would be difficult to sustain. The element of surprise had certainly alarmed the druid-king and his forces; but it was also thought something else may have caught him unawares too, for his counter-attack had seemed delayed.

"We'll need to sound the horns again once our archers are all in place," said Kieman from atop his bay mare.

"And see that our bowmen are not overzealous, lest they unleash their arrows and bolts before our own footmen and knights can pull back."

Kieman nodded in silent agreement. Thus far, they had achieved the near impossible in finally outmaneuvering Kryzol, but the enemy still flaunted superior numbers and also wielded superior weaponry ... one in particular.

* * *

Turi had lost all sense of time as he ascended the path that steepened with each stride of his tiring legs. He scrambled up the rutted trail, stumbling over rocks and slipping on loose dirt, while from the other side of the mount he still heard the clack and clatter of battle mixed in with the shouts of warriors.

And from behind, someone, or something, followed Turi's every move. The silent pursuer kept pace with him as he climbed the side of the castle slopes, never moving whenever the boy paused, always ducking or slipping behind the cover of boulders and thinning trees whenever an instinctive glance back by Turi might have exposed its presence. And seeing nothing trailing him, Turi continued his ascent. It was broken only by an occasional need to stop and catch his breath, or to glance up toward his summit destination — or behind to satisfy himself it was indeed nothing more than just that eerie sensation of being followed.

Turi's forced climb now came in choppier pauses as he worked more frequently to catch his breath. His chest heaved and he bent over, straining to recover from a side stitch that felt like a knife twirling round under his ribcage. The boy moaned, then forced himself to stand, determination winning over pain once again; he turned back for another look eastward over the lower slope trees and the raw morning plain. The distant misty hillocks climbed skyward where the lingering moon hung defiantly on the horizon, as though challenging the rising sun for supremacy. And as Turi's eyes roamed off to the more northern hills, his gaze froze in place!

What loomed there among the peaks made the air in his lungs stop and heave.

A swirl of dark clouds was gathering, taking on a darkly familiar shape. A cold hand stroked his heart as he remembered what he had dearly tried to forget. Turi shut his eyes, the vision of Shaikela in Chinook form and speeding across the tundra toward Narek once again burning a path through his brain. Only now he was not under the influence of a druid's glamour. The horror mustering its strength and shape in the distant hills was one he could not dispel by waking up.

"No!" he shrieked as he turned and scrambled with renewed energy back up the narrow mountain path. Onward and upward he raced with an urgency born of desperation and terror, the ache in his legs and the fire in his lungs defeated now by a mounting sense of purpose. He was less than thirty-feet from the summit, the banked edges of the path rising like bulwarks on either side of him. Turi dared another glance back. His eyes locked onto the northern hills there. A huge, swirling cloud swept along the mountainside and touched down erratically onto the tundra.

Horrorified, Turi spun back around and dashed up the path again. The dagger latched to his hip crooned as though murmuring to him, assuring him he would know what to do once he attained the summit. A gaze upward told him something else. The muscles in his legs shriveled and resisted the forward motion driving them. Turi choked back a scream as his body came to an abrupt halt. For there upon the summit of the warped mountain castle were the hilly cairns that housed Kryzol's great reptilian altar — exactly as they had appeared during the weird Duwin had cast over him days earlier. And perched in a groove cut between the horns of the altar's head, stood none other than the druid-king himself, arms stretched wide in a gesture of supplication.

Turi's entire body shivered as he felt, even from down where he stood, the frosty flood of cryptic energy engulfing the entire summit region and trickling down to him as if in warning. He wanted nothing more than to heed that warning and race back down the winding mountain trail, thus leaving the fool business of challenging the designs of powerful beings like druid-lords and their monstrous creations to men and women of Sir Gaurth's and Lady Jadiane's caliber. But the mere thought of his two gallant friends forced him, however reluctant, into continuing his daring ascent.

And behind him, the one who followed remained fixed upon Turi's erratic dash up the jagged mountain trail.

The path zigzagged left then right. Turi glimpsed the cairns tilting over the high plateau, no more than twenty-feet above him now. He raced round the bend of the banked trail and halted! *A figure loomed directly in his path*: Lothi, scimitar in hand. He was garbed in a maroon robe with a leather tunic wrapped snugly round his narrow chest. His hood was thrown back, his long dust-grey hair flying back in the wind, his pale old eyes dancing with a humorless delight.

"You've been about more mischief than I'd have thought — stripling!" Lothi snarled, one side of his wrinkled mouth curling into an ugly leer. And Turi's long-time fear of the old druid held him riveted to the spot. "Did you really think to have a clear path to the summit?" Lothi twirled his scimitar in a mock salute. Turi took a step back. He glanced anxiously toward the summit, then back at Lothi. The old druid read his face. "Come," Lothi barked impatiently. "Hand over Shaikela's Blade and I'll see you don't suffer the same death as Malbric."

Turi did not respond, the name Malbric not registering.

Lothi frowned, growing more impatient. "Did you think those two armored dolts killing Thayne would be the end of it?" the wry elder added sardonically. "Well they're gone now too."

Turi shook his head in disbelief. That simply could not be. His eyes pressed shut as he fought back tears, then forced them open again, refusing to believe what his mind yet warned him was possible. He stared again at Lothi, whose open hand was now stretched out in anticipation of the Queen's Silver Dagger.

Undisguised hunger, frustration, want, desperation all dominated the old man's face. And that is precisely what Turi saw: a grasping old man. It took no mystical might or cryptic sense to recognize what was now so plainly obvious.

"Traitor!" Turi lashed out in a voice he barely recognized as his own. Lothi withdrew his hand as though bitten. He regarded Turi with a sour sort of awe. The elder blinked, then sneered once more, not willing to acknowledge that this tender little prodigy of Duwin's might dare entertain the thought of defying him.

"'Traitor' am I?" he rasped, the hook-shaped hairs that dangled ridiculously from his nose seeming to twist in agitation. "Well your precious Kathor is nothing more than a dying order of dull-wits."

Turi stared at him contemptuously, annoying Lothi all the more.

The elder druid's rage mounted. "Kieman and Duwin care only for their own meager needs. And they suppress those of us who might ..." Lothi had more to say, but could muster nothing more than soundless gestures. His mouth moved, forming a flurry of words that went unspoken.

Turi stared with a mix of pity and contempt, as one might regard a rabid animal insanely out of control. "And to think, I once feared you," Turi said solemnly, straightening up as he spoke. It was all Lothi needed to jar him back to his former self. He reared up like a spitting cobra on the attack.

"I'll show you fear, stripling!" He waved his scimitar and lurched forward at the very instant Turi yanked out his short sword, again surprising the onetime druid of Kathor. Their swords came together in a resounding clash that echoed loudly throughout the narrow mountain pass. But it was clear from the moment steel met steel, Turi would be no match for the seasoned old druid. Lothi drove him back on contact, sneering at the boy's efforts. "Ho! So Duwin's little pet ... Kieman's pon dares pull a sword on me?"

Turi was knocked off-balance but recovered quickly. He brandished his sword brazenly, surprising Lothi again. "Why fear a wretched old druid who has no Root of his own?" he sneered back.

Lothi's face twisted and he launched another attack. Turi shook as he met the elder's vicious assault, barely having the time to fully realize he was in a life-and-death struggle with someone he had feared his entire life.

And high above, on the mountain-castle summit, Kryzol supplicated to the skies and beckoned feverishly out toward the plain. He held up the modified cone composed of the Roots of his three druids. His eyes burned with a pale blue fury as he pointed and hollered toward the funnel of swirling dark clouds gathering across the early morning tundra.

"Come dear cousin!" the druid-king shrieked, gesturing off in the direction of the two armies battling on the other side of the mount below. "Come put and end to the filth that taints our lands!"

As if in answer to his impassioned plea, the massing Chinook burst up to a height of some thirty-feet and roared toward the figure gesticulating from high on the mountaintop altar. It churned with a sentient deliberation across the plain. Within its vortex of dusty wind and debris, a wispy human image and the warped suggestion of a feminine face formed near its top. It swept malevolently toward the mount.

* * *

Lothi was getting the better of the struggle, even toying now with his lesser skilled opponent, though Turi strove to show no sign of resignation. He would not give this treacherous old devil the satisfaction. But the cunning elder druid was not to be denied and finally disarmed Turi with a deft roll of his scimitar. The young acolyte stood suddenly weaponless, dumfounded in spite of himself.

Lothi sighed deeply, a look of reluctant respect crossing his face. "Well, you've more courage than I'd have thought, brat. Hah! Duwin should have let me teach you this art." He reached out a bony, gnarled hand. "And now I'll have that Dagger."

Turi did not respond. He backed away, glancing again at the summit, then out at the plain. The giant screaming vortex that was Shaikela was halfway across the plain and bearing down on the mountain-castle. Lothi shifted an eye in that direction and sneered.

"Oh yes, she comes, boy ... She comes to destroy Kieman and his meager underlings. As I'd destroy you now if our Lord Kryzol didn't feel you'd be of use to us." He gestured again at the scabbard beneath Turi's tunic. "The Silver Blade!" he hissed.

Turi eyed Lothi savagely, then, ever so slightly, shook his head "no," allowing even a subtle smirk of defiance. Lothi boiled silently then stepped menacingly toward him. And at that moment, Turi tried a desperate end run around the druid, but wound up lurching to one side, his back slamming against the stony bank. Lothi was on him in an instant, moving with an obscene speed and grace for one of his years. He pressed his scimitar savagely against the boy's throat, pinning him in place. With his free hand, Lothi reached down and tugged free the Silver Dagger and its scabbard. The elder druid bristled as a chilly surge passed through him. The cool tingle caused him to shift his grip over to the belt portion of the scabbard.

Turi caught the momentary look of discomfort in Lothi's eye.

"How do you know Kryzol can even use it?" he said, fixing his gaze on the sheathed dagger. "Shaikela forged that Root for her use."

"Kryzol need only keep it from his cousin," Lothi retorted defensively, though not with as much conviction as he would have liked. He glared resentfully at the young pup who still dared defy him. Lothi mustered an unpleasant grin. "And once we've drained her" — he eyed Turi hungrily – "and *others* of their cryptic might ..."

Lothi left the rest unsaid, taking pleasure in the impact his words had on the boy. And Turi trembled, catching their full meaning as Lothi draped the blade belt over one shoulder.

"Druid Lothi, please," he cried desperately. "It's not too late.

Kryzol cares nothing for you. Look what happened to the pons he sent to mine the Marshlands. Do you really think he'll share with you, or anyone else, the power he's after?" Lothi paused, taken off guard, and Turi followed up. "He wants the quicksilver and the strength to use it all for himself! But you can stop him. Be a hero to your own kingdom!"

Lothi's dusty old eyes seemed to soften for the briefest of moments, but too much bile had built up in his soul. He rejected the sliver of doubt that had slipped past his guard and, instead, gripped Turi viciously and started dragging him up the path. "Be a hero to Kieman, eh? So I can go on being his lackey?"

"Then I cannot allow you to keep Shaikela's Power Root," Turi responded with an air of abrupt resolve.

Lothi halted as though jerked by a pair of reins. He drew Turi in close to his face and leered at him. "You cannot? And how —"

He was cut off by a thrumming ... a response to Turi suddenly concentrating fiercely. The Silver Blade quivered at Lothi's side, then sprang from its scabbard, freezing in midair! Lothi gaped in awe — and at that moment Turi broke free of him. The old druid eyed him with shock and a begrudging respect.

"You little bastard!" he snarled, brandishing his scimitar. "Either you —"

And once again Lothi was cut off as Turi ignored him and continued concentrating fiercely. The Silver Blade tilted up so the point now faced Lothi, who, this time, was visibly shaken.

"What Dark Sense lurks inside you?" the elder uttered almost fearfully.

Turi did not respond. His eyes squeezed shut like shades slamming down as he conjured harder, muttering an indiscernible chant. The Silver Dagger moved threateningly closer to Lothi.

Lothi grimaced, then nodded his head in a gesture of acknowledgment: a foe he best take seriously. "Very well, my young druid," he said solemnly, sheathing his scimitar. "Power Root or not, I'm still more than a match for you." The wry elder raised his arms, his gaze fixed on the advancing dagger. And with a wave of his hands, he caused the blade to turn point-upward and freeze in midair.

Now functioning almost entirely through instinct and a natural prowess he barely believed was his own, Turi answered by willing the dagger to turn back toward Lothi. But the old druid countered by commanding it to spin in a small circle and reverse itself so the point now threatened Turi. The energy it took to maintain this mystic struggle was oppressive, exhausting – and Turi felt its draining impact with each attempt to match maneuvers with a seasoned veteran who thrived on it. He could not keep this up for much longer.

CHAPTER TWENTY-SEVEN
An Unexpected Betrayal

Even as the two armies battled savagely at the very foot of Castle Dekras, and even as the cryptic duel on its rear slopes hung in a bizarre balance, Shaikela, in her Chinook form, continued her churning advance across the plain. And Kryzol, ranting from his reptilian shaped altar – the most hideous of Power Roots ever designed – was so fully immersed in his summoning, he held scant awareness of anything else. He knew the lethal Chinook he had created from his cousin's cryptic might was enroute to finish what he had begun. And so he beckoned it on, knowing he needed no other allies once she was upon them.

* * *

A virtual stalemate held Turi and Lothi where they stood, the strain of it wearing far more on Turi. The blade turned his way again, menacing him, but once more he summoned a will from *somewhere else* – somewhere yet unknown to him – and forced it back toward the elder druid. Thus it went with neither gaining ground.

"You've bonded well with Shaikela's Root, young man. Duwin was right about you," Lothi gasped, his tone reflecting an entirely different regard for the youth. "But so long as you struggle here, you'll never reach the Altar Circle!"

Turi glanced toward the summit where Kryzol's Altar loomed above the cairns inside the vast circle of stones. And as he did, Lothi seized that momentary distraction to make another bid for the Silver Blade, this time forcing it to reverse so the pommel was now within his grasp. Turi staggered forward from the cryptic impact!

"It's useless to continue this, young Turi," Lothi eked out persuasively, he too feeling the taxing heat of exhaustion now.

Turi could not utter a response. It was all he could do to keep the dagger from finally breaking free of the mystical tug-of-war and slipping neatly into Lothi's grasp. But how close was Shaikela herself now? Turi risked a shift of his eyes out at the plain to see.

The massive dark funnel bore down rapidly, shrieking as though the dead from the battle on the other side of the mount had all been swept inside it.

Turi and Lothi both fell to their knees, the cryptic struggle wearing them down so only their powers of concentration and will kept the Silver Blade wavering back-and-forth.

"I will never surrender this Blade, Lothi," Turi croaked.

"Then Shaikela won't have it either," the elder uttered.

"Nor Kryzol — traitor!" came a voice that was not Turi's. It caught both of them by surprise. Lothi turned first at the sound.

"Wha ... ?" he snapped.

And Turi turned at almost the same moment. It was enough loss of concentration on both their parts for the mystical dagger to drop to the ground with a loud clang! Both were stunned to see Druid Suhn step out from around the bend flanking Turi. His hood was thrown back, revealing a smooth, youthful face that held no trace of warmth. And now Turi knew he had not simply imagined being followed up the mountain trail earlier.

"Malbric did not die on behalf of one such as you," the lean young druid said coldly, his icy gaze locked on Lothi. The elder druid, already worn down from his struggle with Turi and the Silver Blade, could muster no response or resistance. Suhn closed his eyes and concentrated fiercely. The dagger rose into the air and began spinning erratically. Before either Turi or Lothi could react, Suhn directed the blade straight at Lothi. With no hesitation it plunged into the old druid's heart!

Lothi gave a horrid cry and died frothing at the mouth.

Turi stared disbelievingly at Suhn who was physically shaken from even so brief a use of Shaikela's potent Root. It took a prolonged moment for the tall young druid of Dekras to recover. And finally he walked over and regarded Lothi's corpse almost casually, as though it were nothing more than a piece of rotting wood.

Sprawled close by on the ground, Turi studied suspiciously his rival from the battle on the plain earlier. "And now you will take the Blade?" Turi asked quietly. Suhn turned and eyed Turi as a predator might eye potential prey. He smiled grimly.

"And do what? Bring it to *him*?" Suhn pointed savagely up toward the madly screeching Kryzol, still caught in the throes of summoning Shaikela. He shook his head solemnly. "No, Kathorian. It's yours to take and do what should be done. I saw that out there." He gestured out at the plain and the rapidly approaching vortex.

Turi gazed up at him in confusion. "You want me to ... ?"

"Go ... do it, damn you!" cried Suhn. "I've seen and heard enough by now to know how ill spent my short life has been in the service of that creature!" He gestured wildly again toward the summit where Kryzol stood hunched over the altar, beckoning and calling to the living Chinook now at the foot of the mountain-castle slopes. The wall of stones encircling the druid-king's altar glowed fiendishly. "No more of this," Druid Suhn uttered, more to himself, then turned and disappeared back down the way he had come.

CHAPTER TWENTY-EIGHT
The Root of Power

Turi sat there shivering. He stared at the spot where Suhn had stood only a moment ago, then rose unsteadily, regarding the limp body of Lothi. Slowly, cautiously, he reached down and drew the Silver Blade out from the dead druid's chest, bristling with distaste as it tugged free with a quiet sloosh. Turi turned and eyed the summit resolutely, then ran up the path.

* * *

Kieman and Duwin pressed the army forward, their archers having cleared substantial ground for them in advancing the footmen and knights to the very gates of Castle Dekras. Kryzol's demoralized forces had already retreated to a more defensive position, but now the Kathorians were stymied by the difficulty of trying to storm the bulky fortifications and overwhelm them. Parts of the battle had already pressed past the lower slopes; but the Dekras warriors still held the advantage of a more practiced military discipline and the refuge of the mountainous fortress itself.

* * *

Turi scrambled up the last of the high-banked trail that formed a looping path leading to the summit. Had he glanced back, he would have seen the whirling Chinook at the very foot of the wooded, rear castle slopes, and Shaikela's ghostly eyes peering up at him ... and at Kryzol. But he never looked back or down below again. All he saw and cared about now was what lay ahead of him on the summit plateau.

His body seized with cramps, lungs aching for more air than they could hold, Turi burst out onto the plateau. Looming almost immediately over him was the huge reptilian altar built upon the high cairns and surrounded by the circle of walled rock. He shuddered as he felt a tremendous tug of cryptic energy. He gazed up at the fearsome sight of the druid-king perched a good twenty-five feet above him in the groove cut between the altar's batlike wings. Turi steeled himself, uttered a quiet oath, then sprang toward the rocky circle. And at that same instant, Kryzol peered down and spotted him.

"Foolish pon of Kieman's!" the druid-king hissed, eyes ablaze with a madness born of the cryptic fury he had created this night. Kryzol threw back his head, his black hair flying up in the howling dark wind and icy rain. He gestured down toward the rear castle slopes, his pale eyes every bit that of a madman. "Come dear cousin!"

And in seeming response, the monstrous black funnel churned up the mountainside, chewing up rocks and dirt as it wailed morosely.

Turi clutched the Queen's Dagger in one hand, steeled himself once more — swearing that a noble death here was better than living the life Lothi had chosen — then ran and all but vaulted inside the walled circle of stone.

He was nearly knocked over by the pounding rush of cryptic energy that sailed into him! Panting like a spent dog, Turi gazed up at Kryzol who watched in dark amusement and leered down at him from the altar.

"Now I have you!" the druid-king shrieked in triumph. Kryzol twirled one arm, then whipped it into a pointing gesture at Turi. A streak of fire roared down at the young acolyte, but it was deflected by a maneuver Turi performed instinctively with the Silver Blade. He had raised the dagger and virtually caught the flame, absorbed it, and hurled it back toward Kryzol who barely avoided the return fire!

Kryzol gawked down at Turi in amazement.

Turi himself stared in equal shock at the dagger he clutched in one hand, quite unsure of what he had actually done. He shook his head, drew a breath and permitted himself a smirk of satisfaction. But it was short-lived, interrupted by a grotesque scream from below! The sound was akin to a pair of cold hands gripping him by the ears, forcing them to widen and ingest an overload of noise no eardrums were meant to withstand. Turi dropped to his knees, his knuckles white against his ears.

Below, Shaikela's vortex shape shifted and heaved spasmodically as though in response to Turi invoking her Power Root. Her human essence became more apparent as the tornado form wavered between vortex and wraith, seemingly unable to stabilize itself. Her moon white eyes stared upward, as though appraising both men. And then Shaikela resumed her ghostly ascent, winds blowing devilishly.

From within his perch upon the great reptilian altar's head, Kryzol continued waving his cone and shouting profane incantations into the misty dawn. The ethereal shape of Shaikela trapped inside the Chinook's mass grew more visible, more tangible, as it climbed the mountain-castle slopes. And the rising roar of the wind promised the two on the summit there were nightmares existing outside the realm of dreams. Nightmares that followed where dreams ended.

Turi finally wrenched his hands away from his ears and forced himself to his feet. Once more, from somewhere foreign within himself, he mustered a will that caused him to raise the Silver Blade aloft. And he began chanting, conjuring instinctively in a language he did not know. The blade throbbed, jolting Turi back, but he gripped it more tightly. The sounds of the impending violent winds did not relent.

And then Turi fell silent.

Creeping over the summit was a great ebon figure that towered over everything else on the plateau. It bore only partial semblance to a tornado now as it displayed more the wispy features of a woman's body of gigantic proportions! It writhed and moaned in clear agony. Turi shook in horror as he beheld what the once beautiful Queen of Kathor had become.

* * *

Swept together in mortal combat, both armies halted abruptly, as though a mystic switch had just been thrown. A hush fell over the entire battlefield, the clang and clatter of swords and shields ceasing altogether. The violent activity high on the summit and visible to everyone now, drew all attention that way. Even Duwin and King Kieman fell silent, betranced like the rest, as they stared up at the gruesome drama playing out high above them.

* * *

Shaikela's mixed vortex-and-human form hovered over Kryzol's altar and the circle of stones where the tiny figure of Turi crouched uncertainly, straining to hold the pulsing Silver Blade aloft.

Kryzol himself battled with a growing fear now. His mouth uttered a final soundless command and he nearly melted as a long ghostly arm extended from the stormy mass and pointed menacingly at him. The stunned druid-king recoiled ... then gripped hold of the altar more tightly. Straining for composure, he held up the warped black cone in one hand. He eyed, resolutely, the shifting form of Queen Shaikela.

"You are bound to obey me, cousin. By the power of the sacred union wrought here on this Altar ... you must obey me!" He turned and gestured toward Turi, then down at the battlefield. "Destroy them! I command that you destroy those who violate this Sacred Circle!"

The massive form of Shaikela wavered abruptly, assuming more of its storm shape. The white eyes peered down menacingly at Turi.

"No," he gasped quietly. Shaikela's frosty eyes fixed on the glowing dagger in his hand. The Silver Blade burned white and hot under her glare and all but leapt from his grasp as it fell to the ground. Turi gaped in horror as Shaikela's stormy essence began whirling back into a vortex. He was hurled backward and smacked violently into the wall of mystical stones. He landed in a crumpled heap on the hard rock floor!

And from his perch high above, Kryzol chortled. "Yes ... yes. Destroy them all!"

"No!" Turi countered desperately, mustering one last vestige of courage. He struggled lamely to his feet and drew himself up feebly; gamely. He took several shaky steps toward the cairns, reached down and scooped up the glowing Silver Blade, screaming as a surge of heat ripped through him! Turi fought off the urge to drop it and, instead, raised the dagger and took several more unsteady steps forward so he was now at the foot of the cairns. His entire body trembled fitfully out of control, threatening to collapse in a heap.

Again he held the Silver Dagger aloft.

"Queen Shaikela of Kathor — wife to King Kieman who still loves you! By your own Silver Blade ... have vengeance upon he who has betrayed and enslaved you!"

The whirling mass that was Shaikela stopped abruptly. Her human essence again broke through as her moon white eyes regarded Turi — a flicker of recognition there for the first time. And suddenly the Silver Blade tugged free of Turi's grasp. It hovered in midair, then spun into a tiny vortex of its own.

"No! You are bound to me, cousin!" Kryzol screamed, an undisguised fear in his voice, a sound so seemingly alien from him. "This pon is a liar ... a thief. He sought the power of your Root for himself! Do not listen —"

Kryzol's desperate ranting fell into a panicky gibber as the Silver Blade stopped spinning — and shot straight up into Shaikela's mass! Her vortex slowed so only a whirl of dusty wind orbited what was now the hazy shape of Queen Shaikela herself — a malevolently beautiful figure of frightening proportions. The ashy face turned and stared grimly at Kryzol. And a voice that was more the rasp of a snake lashed out at him.

"Yes, cousin. We are bound once more ... *Come lie with me again!*" The ghostly form of Shaikela leaned over the altar, engulfing Kryzol completely, then whirled back into a vortex. Kryzol cried out pathetically from within, his now feeble voice muffled by the deafening winds of Shaikela's Chinook essence. The cairns that the altar had been built upon cracked and begin breaking up.

Turi backed away, staggering until he tumbled against the stone wall. Within seconds ... Kryzol, his altar, and the cairns were sucked away into the night!

And watching in astonishment from below, cries of fright and awe rose from both armies as the cairns atop the mountain virtually disappeared, followed by a flurry of explosions. Duwin shook his head in stunned silence, while Kieman watched with a mix of horror and agony as his beloved Shaikela roared off into the tumult of the night. And then he lowered his head and wept.

On the summit, Turi shut his eyes tightly and pressed his hands firmly to his ears, his sanity on the brink. The grotesquely howling winds increased as flares of yellow and red filled the misty morning air. There was a roar of thunder followed by a sonic boom! And the summit of Kryzol's Keep disappeared into a rage of explosion and mist that shook the mountain-fortress and the plains below.

CHAPTER TWENTY-NINE
Aftermath

Turi awoke in a sterile white bed ... and stared up in bewilderment. "How ... ? This isn't possible."

Sir Gaurth and Lady Jadiane were looking down at him.

Turi blinked several times, guessing what might have happened. "I am ... dead?"

Laughter filled the room. "Hardly, Sir Druid," said Gaurth. "Though it does seem a miracle that you're not. After what we saw happen on top of that demon fortress."

"But how ... "

Jadiane reached down and put a finger to his lips. "Later, Turi. Rejoice now that we have prevailed. Kryzol is no more."

A voice Turi recognized instantly piped in. "Due to the efforts of one soon to be among the Order of Druids." Duwin appeared at his bedside, smiling. The High Druid of Kathor was flanked by a man and a woman, both dark-skinned and garbed in flowing white robes. Duwin gestured toward them. "You are in a Dekras hall of healing, Turi. This is Paolo and Jezaca. They work here."

Turi eyed the two a tad suspiciously, then twisted his head to see a number of beds filled with patients being attended by other white-robed healers.

"Then it is they who ... ?"

"They first attended to you," said Duwin. "There was another one here gifted enough to care for you while they aided the others. She saw that we didn't lose you."

Turi gave a long sigh of relief and closed his eyes briefly, feeling both flabbergasted and supremely blessed at that moment. He eyed the two Dekras healers again, then quietly reached over and touched them both in thanks. They smiled down warmly at him and departed. "And who is this other healer of Dekras? I would like to give my thanks to –"

A woman's voice – another that he recognized instantly – responded.

"Not of Dekras, Turi." Turi's face could not conceal his shock as he turned to see Kirspen slipping up behind Sir Gaurth. The young Kathorian healer smiled pertly at him. "There will be time to thank me later."

Turi simply gazed up at Kirspen, first in disbelief then finally he let a soft laugh escape his lips. She glided over to him, leaned down and kissed him. Turi's heart danced quietly.

"You are a lucky young man, Turi," said Jadiane.

Turi looked up at Jadiane, then over at Gaurth, and nodded knowingly, in acceptance. He hugged Kirspen warmly then turned to his two knightly comrades. His eyes moistened. "Lothi told me you were both dead."

"Lothi has told his last lie," said Jadiane.

Turi sighed in acknowledgment. With Kirspen's help he sat up in the bed. His eyes pleaded with his next question. "The ... Queen?"

The room fell into silence as Duwin shook his head "no." Turi shut his eyes. "You freed her from her captivity," Duwin added softly. "And Kryzol is gone. His cryptic essence and his body were drawn into the vortex. To where, I do not know. We saw it all from below."

"And Kryzol's army is gone too. They fell into a rout after seeing what took place atop that dread fortress of his," said Gaurth.

"And so did the last of Rojun Thayne's rabble after we slew the first two," Jadiane added. She paused and smirked sweetly. "Of course, Gaurth and I might have caught up to you had this 'manly knight' not been such a burden to me."

Gaurth gave her a playful nudge and, for the first time, Turi found their relationship amusing. Gaurth looked more serious again.

"We had ridden partly up the mountain path ourselves when we met that druid of Kryzol's who aided you," he said quietly.

"Gaurth did not believe him at first," said Jadiane. "He was ready to slay the druid. But then ... then Shaikela came." She stopped, not wanting to speak any further on it.

"There was nothing to do then but seek cover within the rocks. The druid fled. To where, we do not know," said Gaurth.

"He might one day have been my friend," Turi said quietly.

"As many of these Dekras folk might still be — if ours will give them that chance," Duwin added. Gaurth nodded in acknowledgment. Duwin continued. "There are those here who do not bear us ill, and never did."

They all exchanged looks of understanding.

"What has become of ... the Queen?" asked Kirspen.

"We found her lifeless on the summit," said Duwin softly. "And in her true form. We felt it only fitting she be buried there at the site of her triumph. The people of Dekras who have remained will help our soldiers raise new cairns in her memory."

Turi shook his head sadly and wiped a tear from his eye.

Duwin placed a hand on his arm. "At least her soul is freed."

"And King Kieman?" Turi asked.

"He grieves," said Duwin. "But he has the comfort of knowing what Shaikela's death meant. It is up to those who lived to see that the sacrifice made by our Queen is honored."

Turi shook his head in agreement. Again the room was silent.

"Well then," said Duwin more brightly. "We'll take our leave of you now, Turi and commend you to the care of this young healer."

Duwin, Gaurth, and Jadiane turned to leave.

Turi sat up straighter. "I ..." He eyed them all, one by one. "Thank you."

"'Tis all in the line of service — amongst warriors," said Sir Gaurth. He gave Turi a hearty nudge and then departed with Duwin and Jadiane. Kirspen eased over onto the bed next to him and kissed him tenderly. Turi smiled up at her.

"I think I am a lucky young woman," she said, and kissed him again.

THE END.

ABOUT THE AUTHOR

Nicholas Checker has seen a number of his short stories published in literary magazines and has also written a number of stage plays produced throughout New England in such locations as the Colonial Theater in Westerly, RI, the Garde Arts Center in New London, CT, Drama Studios in Springfield, MA, and the Eugene O'Neill Theater Center in Waterford, CT. His published one-act play *Kangaroo Court* (Eldridge Publishing), continues to be performed in various sectors of the country. Making a shift to screenwriting under the guidance of Hollywood screenwriter Peter Filardi, Nicholas developed Nightshade Productions which produced several short films: *Shedim, The Snowman,, Radio Rage,* and *Trashed* — all premiering at Niantic Cinemas and shown at film festivals and other venues throughout the country. He has also written works-for-hire for independent production groups. Nicholas believes his venture into the world of screenwriting was marked significantly by the support of Filardi and his brother Jason, also a Hollywood screenwriter, and the guidance of film studies professor David Tetzlaff. Upon meeting Firesite Films director Alec Asten, Nicholas' script, *The Curse of Micah Rood,* was produced, starring former sitcom star, the late Ron Palillo. It won a number of prestigious awards. Most recently, Nicholas wrote and directed another short film, *Wisp,* currently making the festival circuit. Upon returning to fiction writing, he resurrected an old novel, *Scratch,* and saw it published successfully via Kindle, soon to be out in paperback through Oak Tree Press. *Druids* is his first paperback release.

Made in the USA
Charleston, SC
16 October 2014